'These stories have t[...]
dark, as if spelled ou[...]
an ancient forest'
Ben Loory, author o[...]

'Zarandi splices together the physically grotesque and the narratively experimental – the literary equivalent of that post-punk album that leaves you feeling disjointed every time you listen to it, but which you just can't stop playing'
Tobias Carroll, Managing Editor, Vol. 1 Brooklyn

'Not for the faint hearted... There's an inescapable, violent quality to Zarandi's world [yet it is] tender, funny and moving... Examines the relationship we have with our physical selves and how we learn to exist in our body in this world'
The Idler

'Thoroughly inquisitive and captivating... horror divested of the emotion of horror. Evidently, it accomplishes a nuanced philosophical project'
Heavy Feather Review

Included in Dennis Cooper's best of the year, 2019

SOFT FRUIT IN THE SUN

Oliver Zarandi

Published by Hexus Press

Second edition
ISBN 978 0 9957550 1 7

Copyright © Oliver Zarandi
All rights reserved
Made and printed in Great Britain

Cover illustration and lettering by Bridget Meyne
Design by Bridget Meyne and Thogdin Ripley

Extracts from this work have appeared in the
following places: i-D, Heavy Feather Press, Hotel,
Hobart, Fanzine, Potluck Magazine, Queen Mob's
Tea House, X-Ray Lit Mag.

For my family, always.

CONTENTS

A THREAT

THREAT

"I'm going to move into my mother's skin!" said Grace after her mother died. "She's my mother and I can do what I want with her memory." Many people disagreed but didn't say anything to Grace because they were scared of her.

ARRANGEMENTS

"The house shouldn't be sold," she told Lyle, her brother. "Let me keep it. I'll let her memory and aura continue to live on in the bones of the house."

"What gives you the right to do all of this?" he said.

Grace recounted the days she spent in hospital with her mother. "I kept a tally," she said as she took out a notebook. "I wrote a page a day for every day I spent with her." She took out a small leather notebook and pushed it in Lyle's face.

"I wasted my life watching her, writing in this stupid book," she said. She noted how she cleaned her mother too: the arches of her legs, the small of her back, her buttocks. It was too much. She spent hours looking at her and thinking that, even dying, her mother was twice the woman she was.

TIN

Once Grace's mother had been burnt into a fine powder, she was poured into a tin that once contained tiny biscuits.

Grace carried the tin around with her everywhere. She taped it up tight. "We don't want the dust getting around the house," she told people in the village. "I've already found her covering shelves, books, tables, lampshades, figurines, ceremonial plates."

Grace used to have a glass of wine every evening with the tin containing her mother. She thought about how, yes, this tin once contained biscuits, but then it contained old antique coins and then sepia family photographs.

SHOES

Grace tried on her mother's shoes. They were too big and she never realised how big her mother's feet were.

"Bitch!" said Grace. "Am I always going to play second fiddle to you?" She opened the tin and took a handful of her mother and snorted it up her nose.

"Serves you right," she said aloud to a lampshade.

SHIRTS + WIG

Grace tried to wear her mother's old shirts but they didn't fit either. She ran around the house in the oversized shoes, holding the tin and moved at such a speed that the shirt billowed like a flag surrendering in war.

In those final days of her mother's life, her mother required a wig. Grace took the clippers to her hair and shaved all her hair off and put the wig on. It was a cheap, yellow wig and looked like a bunch of bananas or a pile of sisal rope.

DINNER

She invited friends and family over to the house for an anniversary dinner of her mother's death. She told Lyle over the phone.

"It's only been four months," said Lyle. "But I appreciate you getting us together for this."

But when Lyle arrived, along with his wife, kids, cousins, their partners and a bunch of other relatives, they were worried. The house was filled with photographs of his mother and Grace was talking to all of them angrily.

"Stop looking at me! I'm not copying you."

Dinner was just different types of potatoes.

"Mom always liked them. Skin on or skin off, she liked them," said Grace. Lyle had his head in his hands.

"Why are you dressed like Mother?"

The kids laughed and Lyle hit one of them around the head.

"I feel closer to her this way."

"And the tin, why is the tin there?"

The tin sat atop a chair and even had a plate of food prepared for it.

"You never know."

"What? Never know what?"

"If she gets peckish."

Lyle stood up and said that he was leaving.

HOUSE

"I'm sick of the way you are," said Grace. The tin stared at Grace and eventually broke her. "Tins can't blink, so that's unfair advantage."

Grace took another glass of wine and gulped in one. "You were beautiful, so what. I have my merits too."

Grace had been dumped earlier that evening. She'd been to dinner with the man and she liked him.

But they'd been on several dates now and had had several dinners. "How many dinners does a woman need to eat for a man to fuck her?" said Grace to the tin.

She'd eaten many different types of food with the man. She'd eaten lemon sole and swordfish and moussaka and dupiaza and rump steaks and fillet steaks and lamb chops.

Eventually she got him home. "Take off your clothes," she said. He did and his body was the body of a middle aged man. His belly had a scar across the button that made it look like he'd had something taken out of him.

He told her to get naked too and she did. They had quiet sex. Throughout she noticed he looked disappointed and afterwards, he said that he was.

"You're all air," he said. "Your breasts are a big disappointment, I must say. I was promised fun bags." Earlier on in their relationship she called her breasts fun bags and she regretted it instantly.

"Your mother, now there was a woman," he said. He left. After, she stared at herself in the mirror. She counted everything that was wrong with her. Number one: small breasts. Number two: the vagina hung low and looked like chewing gum on the bottom of a shoe. Number three: too many moles. Number four: dainty feet. Number five: her face. Number six: the tin.

That evening, an oil covered Grace opened the tin, pushed her mother to the side and put in a divider, creating space next to her.

She left the tin in the yard and a note for her brother on top of it: *I would like to be the lesser neighbour*. She held the match and thought that if she did have one good thing about her, it was her decisiveness.

A GOOD AND SIMPLE LIFE

The Boy was born poor and continued to be poor. He couldn't stop the poorness that had infected his family for over three hundred years. He was from bad stock, he thought, a family of beggars and misfits and human footstools, bunion-toed shoe shiners and tumor-nosed accordion players.

"Take a shower," his father used to say, "it might decrease the poorness."

They didn't have a shower, but they did have a bucket and there was water in the river that was near their home. So when he filled the bucket and warmed it as much as he could, he poured the lukewarm water over his skull and came to realise he wasn't getting any richer this way.

His father was a cretin and was covered in boils and his mother was a mute who spent her days pretending to knit. They lived on the outskirts of a large city and everything here was uncomfortable.

"Why are our pillows filled with bones?"

"Because," his father would say, "they are cheaper than feathers."

Ducks did not exist out there and the Boy resigned himself to the fact that he would forever sleep on a pillow of bones until the day he died.

"I live a cursed life," the Boy said to the wind, on his way to school.

Of course, he went to school with other poor children, children who used bad words like *cunt* and *fanny* and said awful things such as *suck my pecker!*

Of course, he was older than the rest of these children. He was 17 and had gangly limbs and a sweaty pubis. He had yellow pimples on his forehead and his cheeks were pumiced. He wasn't good looking.

"Prostitute yourself," his father said once upon a time.

"Ha ha," his mother wrote on a large sheet of tattered paper, knitting those invisible sweaters. "*Prostitute*! He couldn't get raped by a rabid dog," she scrawled shortly after, her writing like a child's.

It was true, the Boy thought. He was in that category of the unwholesomely unattractive.

'You have a good heart though," said a five-year-old girl to him once. She handed him a daisy chain. "But you got the face of an ass."

"Thank you so much," he said, taking the daisy chain and slapping the child across the face.

"To be such a monster!" the Boy would say. He went home and poured buckets of water on his head. If I get richer, he thought, I will be less ugly. And if I'm less ugly, I will live a good and simple life.

His father was outside digging small holes in the soil for no reason whatsoever.

"But it has to be said, son," his father said, stirring his cup of soil, "that wealthy, happy people are fat. And you aren't fat."

"It's true," the mother wrote on her sheet of paper and showed it to the Boy.

"Maybe you need to eat more," said the father.

The Boy was confused. "But we have no food," he said. "What am I supposed to eat?"

"Anything that will make you larger."

And so that evening the Boy ate a part of his bedpost. The wood was soft and rotten and it went down his gullet slowly. He felt the wood settle in his stomach and he imagined eating the bed entire. Maybe his stomach wouldn't digest the bed, but would, instead, become a bed in his stomach where all his hungers would nap and sleep all day.

The next day he wandered the outskirts of the town. He found a dead rat and chewed its meat off until it was just skeleton. He ate the insides of a chair and several newspapers. He broke into an elderly man's home and ate a fridge filled with apricots. He ate so much that his stomach was fit to burst.

"There's no room in my stomach for a bed now, father!" he said. His father was confused.

Several months passed and the son was no richer and no happier. He had gone to bed. His father and mother stayed up and sat next to a fire that they had managed to make out of wood. They stared at each other and smiled. The smiles creased their faces into a million lines and the muscles from their smiles were joined in an unhappy marriage with the muscles on their bony temples.

He woke with a jolt as if he were being brought back to life with a defibrillator. Outside, the land had been covered in a blanket of snow. He jumped out of his bed which wasn't really a bed, but more straw and dung and a pillow of bones, and leapt out into the cold air of what he thought was a Sunday.

"Father," he screamed, "father, if the water is colder and more painful, does that make a difference?"

"Sure," he said. "I shall do it with you once I'm done doing this."

The Boy went over with his pan and started to pour the icy water on his head. It was so cold it burnt and his heart nearly stopped but he kept going. He could see a large castle in his mind and a room filled with gold and women aplenty. He poured the water on his chest and genitals too and the cold seeped under his skin.

"Mother, I feel a change," he said at dinner that evening. They were all eating a potato and a cup filled with soil.

"Yes," she said, "you certainly do feel different." She

blew a kiss over to the Boy and he caught it and put it in his pocket.

BLOOD!

The elderly lady bleeds every day in my favourite café. The owner accommodates this and surrounds her with buckets. He mops it up. Sometimes he puts her in a bathtub, right there in the centre of the café, and she fills it up, laughing and bleeding. People applaud and remark on her unique nature.

I hate her, I tell my husband, I hate her with all my heart.

He says nothing because he's a coward. He carries on reading his newspaper and ignores me. He has beady eyes and untrustworthy hands. He has the bony toes of a medieval Jesus.

I tell him don't you ignore me. Don't you remember my life?

I remember, he says. Your life is one filled with tragedies. I may order another soup.

My parents were two torso-less lugs who beat me silly with rolled-up newspapers. They made me eat sharp foods and made me sleep in difficult spaces, cramming me in suitcases, washing machines, dog houses. Of course, my parents were taller than me, so I only remembered their feet. Mother and her painted toenails, father and his cracked ones.

But I grew up. I grew taller, taller than my parents and I came to know them only by the tops of their heads, two dumb scalps that got smaller with time until they both died of a cancer I didn't care to know more about.

I demanded to know why this old lady was allowed to bleed so freely in the café.

I click my fingers at the owner. Why, I ask, why can she bleed everywhere?

I'm sorry, but she's a regular.

Everybody was afraid of the old lady, I thought. Today, for example, she bled so hard that it came out of her ears, her mouth and eyes and made several toddlers vomit over their eggs.

I turn to my husband and pity him. He's smaller than I am. His hair is a badly formed birds nest on his head, a whirl of thin twigs. To carry on the bird comparisons, may I add that he has a pigeon chest?

We do not get along much anymore. He's a pint-sized intellectual and like most men, he doesn't say he knows more than me, but his eyes do the talking. I sit there and look at him and he can feel me seething at this bleeding old lady and he glances up and blinks twice, slowly, and his lips purse as if to say *shush shush* my darling wife of mine, don't cause a scene.

Don't cause a scene, I say to him. *Don't you know what I've been through in my life?*

He says he does, but the old lady is old and she's rich, richer than us, and there are certain times when we have to allow certain things, times when we must concede and just let it happen.

We go home that evening and I look at our house with scorn. Everything in that house was his decision. The bookshelves, the carpets, the sofas, the ottoman and the paintings, the spice racks and kitchen island, everything. Maybe because my wonderful husband is so small, so miniature, the house is an extension of his body. We go to bed inside his body and I sleep thinking of the bleeding lady and how she is celebrated.

*

The next morning, I decide to see what my own blood looks like, so I take a butter knife and drive it into my arm and twist it this way and that. I'm screaming, but the scream seems so dramatic, so utterly ridiculous that even my husband laughs.

Ha ha! What a terribly witch-like sound, my darling wife, he says as he take the knife and butters a croissant. I realise how ridiculous I'm being and sit down with him at the breakfast table and read the morning news.

A terrorist attack has killed 13 people at a Metro station in Paris.

My bleeding stops but my anger doesn't. I sit there at the table as my tiny husband wears tiny Trotsky glasses, as he reads and his brain gets fat with facts and there I am, ignored, thinking of those people dead at the Metro station, all their blood pooling into some huge jar somewhere in my mind. I feel an agitation in my body and I start shaking. The breakfast table starts to rattle with my convulsions and the toast rack falls down, the eggs on my husband's plate wobble and jump, the tea pot jerks and the croissants shed their skin entirely.

My husband laughs and shakes his head and says 13 dead! Trust the French to moan about such a low number! Try a hundred! Try two hundred! Now that's really dead.

*

We return to the café for lunch. We order sausages and hash browns, coffee and tea and we sit there and glut ourselves on everything in an attempt, I believe, to fill the void that is our lives.

The waiter today looks like a rat with good clothing. His teeth are small and sharp and I wonder if his mother and father have some sort of deficiency.

I'm unhappy with our marriage and I've been masturbating next to your face for 13 years, I say over the sausage to my husband.

That's just great, he says. I'm happy for you. But he's engrossed in the bleeding lady. Everybody is. Chairs are positioned to look at her and people even start to touch her.

The more the merrier, she says in a bathtub of blood. She slams her chubby gout hand on the side of the tub. Bring me a mug, my dry friends! The waiter brings her one and she scoops out a mug full of blood and passes it to my husband.

Drink up little leathery man, she says and he does. She repeats this for everybody in the café and there they all are, drinking this fat wench's blood, the centre of attention.

I stand up and leave the café.

*

I'm in the car and I pass other cars, beeping my horn the entire way. Out of way you bastards, I say and my voice is swallowed in the sound of traffic, the sounds of screaming and talking.

I arrive at the top of the mountain that surrounds the city and I think of that fat bleeding bitch and scream loud and hard, hard enough that I feel my chest go raw and for the first time in a while I feel like I'm being heard, even if it is just the wind listening.

THE HOUSE WAS A CORPSE THAT HAD BEEN BLED DRY

We agreed to meet in a bar known as the 'anus of the city.' It had terrible lighting which obscured its ugly regulars. The regulars had heads like onions with names like Fred, Harry, Deborah, Henrietta. Years of drinking had withered their necks to the size of cocktail sticks and I didn't pity them because I liked hating them. We sat down on two cracked-leather stools and before she could say hello I put my hand out and said, "I haven't made love to a woman in five years and the birth of my children has brought with it a sense of impending dread."

"That's okay," she said, raising her hand also, and I noticed her nails were painted – what did this mean?

Did it mean anything? – "because I am also in a relationship with a man I hate with a passion and have dreamt about other men and women fudging me for the same amount of time."

And to be honest, it was a relief. For weeks preceding this meeting, I had been searching for somebody with the same sense of fantasy as me, somebody who was desperate to indulge in sexual perversions. I went on: "do you wake up sweating, thinking you will die unsatisfied?"

"I do," she said. "The olives here are terrible."

"Yes, they are. I'll order some more." I banged the counter and said *barkeep*! *More olives!* I hadn't been in a bar for many years and had forgotten what level to pitch my voice at. Was I being too loud? Perhaps. I didn't know how to play it cool. My pockets were filled with condoms and small pieces of paper with song lyrics on. I had this idea that if the date was going badly, I would break into song and this would impress her, impel her to stay.

"My kids are called Jerry and Lucille," I said, putting two olives in my mouth. "I used to like Jerry but now he doesn't respect me because his shoe size is bigger than mine. My daughter Lucille, though, I could take her or leave her."

"Will you take her or leave her then?"

"I think leave," I said. "Look, I want to run away with you." She smirked. Was it a smirk? It was a crazy plan. I wanted to ditch my children and wife and take this woman across the country. "I want to run away and fuck you. I want to fuck a lot, you see. I have a lot of plans for how and when I should fuck. Do you? I also want to buy a gun and a large knife and murder people."

"Buy me a drink, lover," she said. Her hair was so long that it reached down and nearly touched the floor. What country was she from? I didn't dare to ask.

"You're exotic," I said. "Do you like it when I say that? Your skin is dark. I'm thinking half Middle Eastern, am I right? Jesus, it's hot in here. Barkeep! Open the window will you?"

There were no windows in there and I ordered two of every drink, a Noah's ark style of drinking. "So what do you say? Would you like to fuck a man like me every day? And murder people?"

"You met me online," she said. "Do you even know my name?"

"Angelina."

"No. It's Maggie. You see? You don't know me."

"But I want to know you. I'm not like other men. I want to take the time to know you."

As a young man, I'd been told I had patience, that I never took too much control. I conceded, my father would say. I was a pushover, he would say. I dated several women and made love in boring ways. I can't orgasm unless a woman's body is in the same position every time. I pump away and think of devastating things. My wife told me I was terrible in bed and that I wasn't a considerate fucker. Okay, I said and we then had two children and I sometimes want to tell them that they are born from the clay of bad sex, slow missionary so as to avoid heart palpitations.

"Maggie, I'm sorry. I am just so... happy we are here together."

She adjusted herself on the stool. "Frankly, you're not my type. You're a little on the ugly side," she said. She wasn't wrong. I belonged with the regulars. I had boils on my knuckles and a nose that people mistook for a cancerous growth. I spoke in a high-pitched voice and cried when it rained.

She told me how she hated men deep down and I tried to convince her that we weren't all bad. We weren't, I told myself.

"But look," she said, raising her glass to her mouth, "I admire what you're doing here. You want me and you want to murder."

"It's true, I do."

"Who do you want to murder?"

"Everybody. Men and women and children. Cats and dogs, too. Fuck reptiles too, I say. Fuck grandmothers and grandfathers. Fuck ducks and geese, horses and fish. I just want to kill. Does that make sense?"

She nodded. "We should start with our lovers."

It was a beautiful moment. I smiled a big smile, teeth and all. She remarked on my gums, the first instance of gum remarking since my mother twenty years prior.

We finished our drinks and I thought of stabbing this great country right in its big fat belly.

I suggested a walk around the park. "We have two legs, we can walk," I said. "That's more than some. Some people have their wheels. Others are stuck indoors forever. But not us – the world is our oyster." I thumped my legs and flexed my bicep, hoping she would see it. "I can lift that bench over there," I said and the sentence died as it hit the air, conscious of my own lameness, my utter weakness.

So we left the anus of the city and walked out into the cold night air. It smelled of sewage that evening. The city always smelled of something rotten and every day was a revelation in that way.

We walked around using our legs. We breathed the park air in through our nostrils and spoke about how we would murder our lovers. We thought of bludgeoning, of strangulation, buggery, setting them on fire, shooting them between the eyes, slitting their throats. We saw a couple being carried around by a horse and carriage and the horse looked depressed and worthy of death.

The evening came to an end. We kissed on the lips and I said goodbye, see you soon. I walked home with a semi-erection.

When I got home that evening, even my front door depressed me. The creak of it, the colour. All of the family photographs too, the ones of my wife, her face so spiteful and my two children holding rackets and balls in carefully held poses. Everything in the house was upsetting. The walls were sad and the carpets looked drained of life. My house was a corpse that had been bled dry. But I took my clothes off with glee and thought of Maggie and her gusto.

I went to bed and slept next to my wife who snored for many hours. I said *hello my love* and she said *hmmmm*. There was a funny feeling as I held her. I knew I wouldn't call Maggie back, but she would join the other women I had met and they would all be pushing me on to be the best man I could be.

STAGING OF ACCIDENTS

1

Ballard left the city to live a life in the wilderness. He wrote a letter to his wife and two children in which he vowed never to return to the life of the city or speak to people again.

He wrote the letter by dim candlelight. The city was quiet that evening. He could hear the scratch of the pen against the paper. In the distance, one could hear an ambiguous wail, an open mouth of a man or beast in pain.

He left his wife sleeping in their bed. He kissed her head. He went to see his children for the last time and kissed them both on their heads too.

He was sad but driven by some inward force.

He roamed the house and touched the furniture. He held his armchair and recorded its touch in his head. He slid his hand across the marble mantelpiece above the fireplace; his hands, upon inspection, were covered in a light film of dust, the skin of himself, the skin of his family. He wished he could package this dust and take it with him.

Before he left the house, he checked his bags. He had packed clothes for every season, a grooming kit, a rifle, bullets, hunting knife, medical provisions, tinned food and binoculars. As he exited the house, he closed the door to but did not lock it. Upon leaving, he entertained thoughts of his family being assaulted in the dead of night by a faceless assailant. He thought of his bloodline being ended there in the house he had left. He left the house bearing ill feelings towards the ones he loved.

2

The thin man did not make enough wages to sustain his life in any meaningful way. In the same way a human puts food into their mouth, chews, swallows and devours food, the air of the city consumed the thin man little by little.

For fear of anything happening – a fall or perhaps a social encounter that raised the heartbeat – the thin man confined himself to his chair most evenings.

From the chair, he saw the city down below. It was a city in its infancy. Flaws were being ironed out. The inhabitants were testing limits, boundaries were pushed and sin was apparent everywhere, the windows steamed up and hidden from his view. Food was scarce in his apartment. Often he would lick the tips of his fingers and dab the breadcrumbs off his plate one by one to make them last longer.

To keep warm during winter, he would have to wrap his feet in torn bed sheets.

He would pace the apartment to keep the blood flowing in his veins.

One evening, he happened to notice a woman in the apartment across the road. The mould lining his windowpane obscured his view of her. He found a cloth and wiped it clean. The sky was dark and so was his apartment in order to save money on electricity. By candlelight he watched her walk in and out of view. His chest raised and rattled, his ribcage shrink-wrapped by skin.

She was a beautiful woman in a rugged way. From a distance, he could not quite make her details out. Was she brown or blue eyed? Were her hands big or small? How many toes did she have? He invented it for her. He wished her to be full blooded. He imagined holding her hands and feeling their warmth against his cold.

Her legs, too, were strong and muscular. This is what he wanted to believe. But all he could make out, from distance, was her hair scraped back into a bun, her eyes downcast and cheeks ruddy, her posture in a permanent downward pose, a supplicant, but a supplicant to whom? Did she live alone? Was there somebody else in that space that loved her? Or perhaps hated her? That, perhaps, gave her orders?

The thin man loved her, from a distance. Over time, he spoke at the window, to her. He wondered if she could hear him. He wondered if she was doing the exact same thing.

After a few weeks, the thin man realised that maybe she was a woman or maybe she was new mould, delicately placed in his line of view.

3

The next day the boys all signed on to the *Cannery World*. Their names were Adam, Grainger and

Kenneth. They were set to sail the next day.

They introduced themselves to the other sailors. They were pale and sickly looking young men with weak handshakes. Adam shook hands with a man who called himself Jerky and nearly broke his wrist.

The hall where they were all stationed was high and wide, the brick blue, the windows tall and domed at the top. Kenneth wondered if it was once a library in here, a fine place for knowledge. The hall had the faint smell of ammonia, which made the boys feel sick.

Grainger, the skeptic, was unsure of the crew they had fallen in with. "There's something in their eyes," he said. "Like a fever. A feverish look."

Adam looked around, his head lowered and hands behind his back like he was bobbing for apples. "The one who calls himself Jerky," he said, "had the handshake of a child."

"We can't judge a man by his handshake," said Kenneth. "They're just like us, I am sure of it."

The next day, the *Cannery World* set sail. Adam asked Jerky where they were headed. "We're off to discover new worlds," said Jerky. "We're off to find out terrible truths."

Down below deck, Kenneth noticed that some of the boys he was bunking with had started to fall ill. A ginger-haired man with a concave chest started becoming short of breath. Kenneth and his roommate wetted a flannel and place it upon the ginger man's forehead like a portion of fish.

Kenneth asked him a question to pass the time. "Your name, chap?"

"Wallace," he said. He grimaced in pain and pointed to his crotch.

"What's this? You hurt? Down there?"

Wallace nodded.

Adam and Grainger walked past and came in the room. They helped Kenneth remove Wallace's trousers and pants. His penis was covered in small, yellow lesions. From his urethra, a green liquid secreted. The shaft of his penis, too, was covered in broken capillaries that contrasted against the sickly jaundice of the penis's skin.

Soon enough, nearly the entire crew had come down with this mysterious illness. The men who were not afflicted had holed up in the mess hall. Grainger and Adam were amongst these men.

They had barricaded the doors, thinking of tomorrow. Grainger asked where Kenneth was.

As they looked down the corridor, they saw Kenneth and Wallace, both up against the wall, perfectly in tune with each other, moving inside of each other.

Grainger trembled, contemplating on whether or not to remove the barricades and enjoy the freedom they had been granted, stranded in the ocean with no civilisation in sight.

4

These were exciting times. This year, no new films were released. No new species were discovered and nor were there any disasters or acts of terrorism or demonstrations or charges of corruption. The world was at a standstill.

Things had simply stopped. People had stopped having sex. No new children were born. Children had stopped playing. The sun sometimes refused to go down and the elderly were cooked on the streets. In Los Angeles, they were flattened against pavements, burnt, singed, and the authorities had not bothered to clean them up.

So when people get excited, I have to remind them

that last year was a year of unpredictability. This year, yes, is different. But next year, too, will be different. The excitement will stop. Creation and malevolence will begin again.

5

Thirty days later and she was still stuck in the quicksand. She held onto the branch of a tree, which saved her from sinking completely, but did not have enough purchase upon the branch to escape. She imagined herself as having longer arms, but sunk lower, thus putting herself in the same position as she was now. She imagined herself as a man and this, too, gleaned no further solutions.

6

We were young. George kidnapped the dog from next door. He stuffed it into a bag. We went to the woods and played with it. We cuddled it. It dirtied our clothes.

There are some thought processes that, as an adult, are difficult to rationalise. The thought processes of a child seem automatic, as if carried out by a somnambulist.

So when we took the dog, placed inside the bag and tied it up, we weren't thinking. In the woods, a rock face – grey, cold – triggered something in us and we decorated it with the dog.

7

My wife found the email. We shared an email account and had a folder each. The email was asking me if I'd like to subscribe to 'cum eaters'. She asked me what it was and why I was searching for cum eaters. I told her it wasn't me.

The same thing happened the week after. This time it was asking if I'd like to renew my subscription to 'A Black Man Is Fucking My Daughter.' There was a picture of a long, brown penis in the headline image and the title was printed in red writing on the penis.

Again, she thought all this pornography had died down. But a few weeks later, I got the email to confirm my username 'bignuts' for a local cream pie meet up for over forties widows.

My wife left me and it was then that I decided to email the correct people and thank them for their help and suggestions.

A MINIATURE TALE OF MOTHERHOOD

My children are cruel and look like goblins. Every day they take something away from me and I don't ask for anything in return.

I asked them this morning, "What do you want for lunch?"

"Your breasts," they said.

So they had them. They suckled my teats, one apiece, and sucked them dry. No more milk. And then they took turns chewing them off.

"I'd like those," I said. "I'm single. Men are fickle

beasts, children, and find two breasts attractive, one less so and none a travesty."

They said nothing because they were young children, little Ronald and Maisy, but they shot me with devilish smiles nonetheless.

And then years later, there was nothing but growth. The children grew larger day by day and started to outgrow rooms and houses. I was married to another man at this time, Thomas, and wanted desperately to make things work.

"The children are too large for this place," I told him.

"Then we must uproot once more," he said. And so we did. We went to a larger house in the countryside where my son and daughter could easily fit in rooms.

They grew to be spotted beasts in their teenage years and they would shed skin all over the house.

"Tidy up," they would say and I did. I did everything I could to keep the house in order. They would cry tears that drowned several household animals. They shed enough skin that we used it as bedding for our horses. When they popped spots, the pus would coat the room a delightful yellow.

By the time they were 18, I was altogether used up. I

was a drink that had been sipped at and then refilled and sipped at and refilled. I was broken crockery. I was a wedding dress with holes in it. I was Miss Havisham's dining table.

I would sit in the sitting room, for that is what it's there for, and tell Thomas how sore my legs were. He didn't hear me, though, because my breasts had been chewed off in my youth. And there I was, then, staring at my withered legs and arms and torso and, just to compound this, I had a hand mirror where I could stare into my hollowed-out face and comment upon it in negative, cruel ways.

My husband died. It was a tragedy, yes, and my children came to the funeral with me. It was raining that day and I cried so much that the tears ran hard down my cheeks, hard enough to create rivulets in my skin.

My children could not cry. "Mother, lend us your tears," said Maisy. She was a giant now and I spoke only to her shins. Ronald was even taller, his head covered by tree leaves.

"Here they are children," I said, cupping my hands and handing them tears, all my grief for my husband passed onto them.

And so they cried and then they left. I didn't speak

to them for many years and it must be said that they didn't ask anything of me. But I called them. I called them every day. I left messages. I wondered what had become of them. Ronald had surely never fathered children, considering how monstrously ugly he was and perhaps due to the size of his genitals, which now needed an entire house to themselves. And maybe Maisy was a mother herself now, but who would climb the ladder to her giant vagina? Nobody, I imagined.

I sat there in the large country house, my legs two tiny cocktail sticks. I crawled to bed every night. I could have stayed bedbound, but I didn't. I made a point of this. I read books and ate simple food from my garden. I dug my hands in the soil and dragged up raw potatoes and carrots. I ate worms. I ate snails.

But today, things took a turn for the unexpected.

My hair is now grey and barely covers my scalp. I am a body that has rivers, deep and wide, running down it. I sit there naked and see my giant children approaching, wondering what they are going to take from me now. They walk straight towards the house and are as tall and wanting as ever. I welcome it with open arms.

CELLO

My husband left me for a pile of bricks. I loved him for two years but we'd been married for ten.

When we first met, he was a beautiful man. He had strong cheekbones and played the cello. I always said to my mother that I'd marry a cellist and when I did, I met her for coffee, stuck my tongue out at her in an act of defiance and said fuck you!

The hair of a mop, the eyes of a methadone addict. His fingernails were feminine and often painted and his abdominal area reminded me of an ironing board. His mouth was like the opening of a conch shell.

He owned many pleasant mahogany items, which he sometimes let me run my fingers across. He also liked to buy objects made of marble and would, on Sundays, go around the house and touch every marble object before going to bed. I can see him now walking around the house, touching the top of a fireplace, a cherub's penis, stroking a miniature column.

But living with a cellist is not the same as dreaming about cellists and perhaps I should have realised this sooner, but men never live up to their profession. Perhaps the cello itself seduced me and, yes, maybe I should have married the instrument and not the man.

My husband was cruel in the first year of our marriage. He impregnated me against my will. I didn't want the baby to grow inside of me but it did and it grew there for nine months and it had the gall to get bigger, too.

During those nine months, my husband played cello all day and all night without socks or shoes. He wore corduroy trousers and a corduroy shirt and I wanted to tell him that this was not okay, but I said nothing. I focused on my body.

The baby was about to be born, and we had to erase an important room in our house to accommodate it. So we decided to get rid of the library, the walls lined with books and memories, and in the baby would go. I grew to love the idea of the baby the same way one's tongue grows to love the taste of a vegetable you once hated as a child.

*

My husband noticed that after the birth, I started to become ugly. He pointed out that my vagina had lost its shape. Your hair, too, he said, is falling out, he'd say.

Your toes are still bloated.

Your breasts are constantly sad.

You have old woman veins on a young woman's legs.

He compared me to a ship containing treasure during a tempest. There is a beauty there, he said, but it's lost for all man to appreciate.

You're a shipwreck.

And so after two years, love turned to nothing. I actually thought love was a thing, a physical object. I started looking for it in our house. I looked under the sofa, under the bed. I upturned the ottoman and looked there too. I looked in jam jars, butter dishes, raisin bowls, mugs, glasses, chiffoniers, beds, cupboards, steam trunks, washing machines, boxes, bins, ovens and attics.

*

When I was a young girl I tried my hardest to look like a woman. I put on make-up and wore high heels and bras. I moved in provocative ways in front of the mirror, movements I had learnt from television and spying on women, women who were older than I was, and I even looked at my own genitalia with the eyes of another, judging myself, thinking, yes, this is good and yes, this is a woman.

The house I grew up in was a house of foreignness. My father was a translator and my mother was a writer. Our house was filled with books with thick spines and golden lettering, some of which I ran my fingers up and down on.

I would tell my mother of the boys I was in love with and she would sit at the kitchen table peeling various fruits – apples, pears, oranges, blood oranges, kiwis – with a small but sturdy knife and she would always lean into the chair and slouch so her legs were spread and she looked dirty and sluttish.

Mother, I love Brian. Brian had ginger hair and ginger freckles and according to the children at school, he wore the clothes of other, dead children.

Mother I love David. David had webbed feet and we thought, but perhaps incorrectly, rickets.

Mother, what I love about Mark is his passion for milk. His passion for bugs and small animals, his tender hands and foppish ways.

Of course, she dismissed all of these boys with the wave of a juice-drenched hand.

Your father, now there is a man.

He has good flesh and gives off a charming odor. He bites my neck and knows the way to an orgasm without a GPS. Your father talks and I listen because he is a man of respect and good bone structure.

I walked away with my head down, defeated and my lungs pricked with a feeling I couldn't quite put my finger on.

*

I gave my child away to science and left my lonely house.

At the time, I lived in the city and the memories of my husband, the cellist, were everywhere. I couldn't walk past a park bench without thinking of him, about that time we kissed on it. The bench was dedicated to a Persian poet, and I noticed that every bench was named after the dead. I started to block out entire streets from my daily walks because we had both walked along those routes. Entire streets, benches, cafes, parks, everywhere, everywhere had become a series of places I couldn't return to.

I decided that relationships are a series of places that you can't return to.

And so with a pen and a map, I marked out where I could and couldn't go. Entire sections of the map were marked red. I remember the streets that we walked down, hand in hand, he carrying a book on cellos, me carrying a freshly cooked sourdough. Other streets were erased because I thought of him there. Like the fountain behind that Georgian building, the fountain that was apparently the cause of a cholera outbreak and I saw a picture of a cholera victim, blue, sad, and thought of my husband. Even the cholera fountain had to go.

Life had become an act of whittling. Life before was like a large tree, I thought, for want of a better metaphor. And then, over time, I started cutting the branches off, chipping the bark, chipping it away, yes, and then chopping the top off to make the whole thing easier and then the shaving started, shaving it thinner and thinner until it became nothing at all and, in fact, to return to the reality of the situation, the map was all red, all except my house and then that was red too.

I couldn't stay there. I went out and spoke to a group of local vagrants who sat in the alcove of a derelict building, soiled bed sheets, pots and pans, tins of food and I told them that my house was now their house. The vagrants moved in and I moved out.

*

I had infected our house.

Somebody did say I was infectious once, so perhaps it wasn't farfetched to think that I'd made my house sick.

The sofa got the flu and sneezed up phlegm on my Persian rug. The lampshades got meningococcal septicemia and became covered in sores, red and black. The globe where I kept liquor got macrocephaly and became so big I had to leave the room. My bed got cancer and didn't accept me anymore. The wallpaper began to peel off the walls because it was depressed and, eventually, my microwave got dementia and forgot to cook the lasagna I'd put in it.

There was the sound of the cello, too. It wouldn't go away. For each dream I had, there was a cellist creating the soundtrack to it; a slow, droning music that echoed in my head even after waking up.

*

I purchased an old farmhouse.

I went to the local landowner and purchased it with the money I'd found under the sofa.

The house was empty. The walls were bare and there wasn't any furniture. There was a dead owl in the fireplace and I observed the majesty of its feathers before tossing it onto a homemade pyre.

One of the bedrooms was painted mustard yellow and another was painted the colour of vibrant ham.

The view outside my window reminded me of my dreams. If you want to know, there were trees, tall and thin, and some had leaves and some didn't. The hills were round and lumpy.

For a while, I slept on the cold floor and wrapped myself in a small blanket that I'd found in what used to be a guinea pig hutch.

I remember the noises as if every living thing had been wired with a microphone to my brain. I could hear the blackbirds singing and the spiders crawling through the grass, every leg, and the sounds of foxes rutting, the pain of coitus, air.

*

And then the men started coming to the house, men with different bodies and different accents.

There were big men and small men, fat men and thin men. Men came with white skin and black skin. Some men had no skin at all. Skeletons. One of the men wore a fez, the other a fedora and a cigar. Another man came with a tape measure and insisted I measure him limbs, organs, circumferences.

The short men came in groups, for fear the taller men would wipe them out with their clubs hewn from strong forest wood. The taller men, too, were often wary of the packs of short men and had darting eyes.

There were the men with the big mouths whose stories of personal struggle could be heard over the treetops.

One man said: my mother loved me too much, which is why I'm so caring.

Another said: I was born in poverty and now I'm rich but no happier.

And also: I was born with a gift and this gift produces more life, and piss.

The house that I bought was empty but thanks to these swathes of men the house was slowly filled with furniture, a plumbing system, paintings – usually their own portraits – carpets, paintings, potbellied stoves, pet animals.

I smiled but didn't ask for this. One of the men came up to me and said: So, what do you say? I said: What do you mean? And he looked at the hundreds of men surrounding the house, each holding a gift and he laughed and said what do you say to all of this? To which, of course, I said I don't know. And, to which, of course, he replied: you were meant to say thank you.

*

There they were, camped outside my house. They would come and knock on my door and ask how I was settling in.

Just fine, thank you.

A Tatar with a white hat danced a dance for me and handed me a puff pastry. Enjoy, he said and ran off into the forest where, undoubtedly, the other Tatars were camped and watching me with a collapsible telescope.

*

My body started to improve. My stretch marks magically disappeared or perhaps I just wasn't looking at them; or that maybe people weren't pointing them out anymore. And my feet had returned to their former size and no longer a point of ridicule amongst the men. My breasts were the same. My hair was no longer falling out and, again, maybe this was because there was none left to fall out.

It all fell out over a number of years and left me with a shiny head and a penchant for purchasing wigs.

*

There was no sex, although the men offered to move into my vagina as if it were a house. Can we move in, they said. It's cold out here and probably much warmer in there.

I said no. This house is not for sale. It's not up for rent, either. In fact, this house is abandoned and empty. There's a box of toys in the house and they're from a time before we were born and over the box is a muslin cloth and nobody's touched these toys in years.

*

My body wasn't my body but a film. My eyes were cameras, 35mm cameras, and looking at my hands I thought: these are not my hands, but a moving image of what my hands look like. The same for my face in the mirror; it was like the first person had become the third person.

There *she* is.

There *it* is.

It's not happy.

And this continued for some time. I became a character in the house and watched a life unfold.

I watched, as it was cooked dinner by other men. I watched it receive kisses in locked bedrooms and saw it getting undressed, positioned carefully by the bedroom window with the lamp illuminating just enough of its body – the curve of its back, buttocks, a nape – so the men camped outside could watch.

It was a body with an audience with perfect grammar.

*

The men complained of injuries, others of grievances suffered throughout their lives.

I broke a toe, one said.

My wife left me for a younger man who looks the same as me, but better in almost every single way.

My wife left me for herself, who she said was better than I could ever be.

66

I became tired of listening to the men. I had listened to my husband for ten years. I listened to other boyfriends for years, too. I tried to think of how many hours I'd spent listening to men and created a pie chart in my head illustrating the ratio of time spent enjoying my life and time spent listening to men.

I thought of all the men who had used me for various things in their life: for talking at; for sex; as a punch bag. Looking at childhood photographs, it is interesting to see vitality in my eyes. Now, however, you could say some bulbs had blown in my vessel. I was tainted. I'd been handed around too many times. I was like an object that once had vibrancy but over time and with wear and tear had become dulled, blunted and ultimately nothing.

When all the men had gone to sleep and my doors were locked, double- and triple-locked, I sat in my bedroom with the lights off. Out there were the dying embers of the men's fires and I could just about make out their eyes, open and staring back at me.

No matter where I go or where I travel, those eyes will be staring at me and their fires will not die out.

*

Sometimes the men danced. They danced into the night and made whooping noises. Some men got undressed. It was usually the fatter men who did this and their buttocks looked like battered pillows.

The men would become drunk and haunted in their eyes. Sometimes they'd storm the house but thankfully they provided me with barricades only hours before in case of such an emergency.

*

My breasts can fit several pens underneath them. I don't need a penholder. And then my feet; my husband said they were large – even larger when the baby was on its way. Look at the size of these, he'd say and I'd say nothing. I'd smile a big wide smile that was fake and looked like I needed the toilet. He used to turn me over and investigate me. Look at this, he'd say. A prod. Look. And it was a spot on my spine. How does a woman get spots on her back? I don't know I said and I was still smiling even though it wasn't really a smile. How does a woman get a spot on her back? And here too. He prodded just above my anus, which was unshaven and shabby – his words, not mine – and there was a spot there too. I was covered in spots. He said I was a shipwreck again and again and that my body was sinking treasure. I smiled and smiled and smiled.

Learn things too, he said. I play the cello, what do you do? I read. He said learn this, learn that. I did.

I learnt about burn marks on bodies. I learnt about plastic surgery techniques and how people learnt to use prosthetic fingers after having them crushed. I learnt things for him. I learnt the cello. I learnt about castrato singers. I was a fountain of knowledge and full of beans. His words not mine.

*

In fact, the act of swallowing had become a problem, which we shan't get into but I basically had to count to three before swallowing, like taking a leap of faith, and only then did the water or soup go down my throat.

The men had no problem eating and I watched them, jealously, as they skinned rabbits, cooked rabbits and ate rabbits. The men were constantly fat with gin and here I was in the house alone, counting to three and creating new superstitions and new rules to impose upon myself, as if I couldn't sink any lower.

*

The men now reside in my house and my body and when I talk they tell me to be quiet and be beautiful and they tell me my faults and I smile and I sink to the bottom of the ocean and they watch my shipwreck surrounded by sand and seaweed and sharp, jagged rocks. They stroke my hair and I say nothing and sometimes I purr because they tell me to. Their eyes search for my treasure but their eyes are tired, but I know their eyes will not stop looking at my shipwreck, that their eyes will not die and I think of the quicksand and, yes, that maybe I should sink. All their language became foreign the lower I sank. My ears would fill with liquid and all I heard were the languages of savages, foreigners, sounds.

*

I remember when I first met my husband, the cellist. It was in a café. People sat in the café facing each other and, perhaps, staring through each other at other cafés, thousands of miles away where the exact same action was occurring.

We also sat staring at each other. We'd met outside. So perhaps it's safe to say we didn't meet inside the café, but outside the café. Now we were inside and two black coffees sat beneath our chins.

I went to talk but he was first and said let me tell you about life and pain.

I smiled.

And then I said, okay and listened.

COW

Some people lose things in the war, he said. Legs, arms, eyes, ears, scalps, nipples, cocks, balls. I didn't, he said. Was this boasting? He moved the saltshaker back and forth, not in a way that suggested mental instability but perhaps boredom. The food arrived and he dissected the steak. I didn't lose anything, he said. Is that right?, I said. That's right. I gained something, he said. I gained the power of the American army. I have the American army in my belt. My eyes, too. Look into my eyes, he said. I did. My eyes are made from artillery lenses from China, he said. Every night I dream that I'm in a plane, fighting clouds. He didn't say anything else for the rest of the meal, though was it really a meal or just two people sharing a table to eat a cow at?

A TRAGIC LIFE

I sat down in front of my date and told him that I have lived a tragic life through the pain of others but have never encountered drama myself.

We met online over a paid dating app for intellectuals. I paid forty pounds a month for this and hadn't had sex once.

My date was called Warren and his head was round. I liked a man with a round head. I also heard that a large forehead meant that he was clever, but perhaps I have been lied to.

Warren chose the restaurant. It was the French word

for atmosphere, which I think is just atmosphere. The tables were small and wooden and the chairs were uneven. Somebody next to us ordered a carafe of wine but pronounced it *cuh–raff-eee*.

I ordered a starter that was light on substance for fear of choking.

Why has your life been tragic?, he said with a wry smile. And I mean it when I say wry. He nodded his head as he said it. I think that he thought he was in a Woody Allen film. He always looked like he had cameras trained on him. He wore corduroy trousers and a linen shirt, as if that makes any difference.

I said my friend was killed when I was 18.

    That's awful.

The meat on his face dropped. Warren looked like a dead person.

But he played ball.

    And when was he killed?

    She.

    How was she killed, sorry.

She was found in seven different plastic bags.

Okay.

The police caught the killer mid-disposal.

As in?

As in, he was throwing my friend away.

It felt weird to say that, that my friend was being thrown away.

And what was your friend's name?

Amelia.

Nice name.

It is, isn't it?

I took a bite of my starter which was several rocket leaves weighed down by salt flakes and pepper.

How did it happen?

She was drunk and needed a lift.

Right.

And she thumbed him down.

The killer?

Yes. And she got in and he took her back to her place.

Right.

And then he drugged her.

Right.

Took her back to his place.

Right.

And the rest is too much to talk about.

Right.

He ordered another bottle of wine. The waitress came over and she showed the bottle of wine to Warren and he nodded and she poured out a little bit for him to try. Warren needed this time, I think, to recover from the story of my friend being butchered.

Which of course wasn't true. I didn't even have a friend called Amelia.

He raised his glass. To Amelia, he said.

I raised my glass too and half-heartedly said yes, to Amelia and clinked his glass in reply.

I'm looking forward to these scallops, he said. I've heard only good things.

I was surprised at Warren's attempt to change my date in a direction he felt comfortable with. This is what men did. They try to steer the date into smoother waters, waters they are comfortable with.

Your friends tell you good things about seafood?

Yes, I guess so.

As in you read a review?

I did.

Was it a good review?

He was sweating.

It was a good review.

Did it get five out of five?

No.

Four?

Yes.

That's very confident of you, I said.

What?

Taking me to a four out of five restaurant.

I just heard about the scallops...

But what about me?

Please, he whispered. I believe that he pleaded here.

The main course arrived. He smiled at the food like it was a friend who had saved him from a particularly awkward encounter. I looked at my food like it was medium rare steak, which it was.

Why else is your life so tragic, he said. He was, at least, trying to return control of the ship to me.

I said my mother was murdered too. And that my sister was killed too. And that most important female figures in my life had been disposed of by men.

I didn't go into details about these murders. He didn't

ask either.

I ate a piece of prosciutto ham and choked on it. I knew it would happen. I put my hand in my mouth and felt around for a stringy piece of fat and pinched it with my thumb and forefinger, pulling it out like a miniature rope.

He looked disgusted, which was fantastic.

So, he said. He grunted. He moved in his chair. So, what do you do for a living?

I couldn't believe it. He had ignored the display of vulgarity. He had ignored the miniature rope of fat being pulled from my throat.

I told him that I was the manager of a waste disposal company which was not true either. I wanted to sound as boring as possible. I wanted to wear him down and melt him there and then at the table.

That sounds interesting, he said.

Unbelievable.

I told him I got pregnant but when it came out it was just grey water and ears.

Nothing.

The rest of the meal passed without anything else of note occurring. He paid for the meal, of course. He tried to hold my hand when we got outside, but I refused to do so.

You've got small hands, I said.

I hit him where it hurt, it seemed. He looked at his hands.

Have I?

Yes.

Well, you know what they say.

I *do* know what they say.

He blushed. His cheeks looked like somebody had smashed beetroots into them.

Would you like to walk through Soho? Maybe get a drink?

I said I guess so. I put on the most spiteful face I could.

Warren took me for drinks and I told him more horror stories about myself. I told him things I liked about men and how he would never achieve any of those things I liked about men, that his mission tonight was impossible.

Warren smiled the entire time.

He came back to my place and I even opened the door for him. He entered my flat first. He took a seat on the sofa. He took the initiative. I wanted to vomit.

I was, however, quite prepared for a man like Warren. He had control of the ship. All men think this because they are men. But as he sat there with his round head and little hands, I thought many thoughts, thoughts that were, in my head, not words but actions, thoughts like I hate you, I hate you, I hate you.

THE CHAIR

Somebody has replaced my chair with a child. It was a beautiful chair, a rocking chair fashioned by my father.

Though, of course, one mustn't give credence to anything in this town. The town has a population of God-knows-what and its name does not interest me much either.

The child is a genius. It's dressed in a purple smoking jacket. It has sandy hair and wears corduroy trousers. It's rosy-cheeked and doesn't remind me of my own uglier children.

It was smoking a pipe. The smoke filled the office.

It also filled the lungs of my employees. It managed to aggravate my lungs, too. I coughed three times. I put my hands to my mouth to halt the germs from escaping my vessel. I coughed again.

Look, on my hand: tar-coloured phlegm. The employees, they begin to leave. I only have two employees. Their names are Suskind and Clyde. They are immigrants. Suskind is Danish. Clyde is African.

Clyde was his name because somebody had called him it. When he was born, he wasn't given a name. He told me, once, that when he was born, the only thing he was given was the curse of life.

Clyde was a depressing fellow to be around.

In many respects, I am glad to see them go. The child says he is glad too. I point out that he doesn't know them from Adam. The child scolds me for using Adam, not God.

The office isn't really an office. It is a hut, of sorts, constructed from oak trees. This hut, it was built by my father. His name was Gottfried. He was of German descent. He came to America to forge his own path.

Notice the use of was, not is. He *is* dead. He died due to an accidental poisoning. It was on a summer's day. I remember this clearly. He was playing the goat for us children. Fooling around, you could say. And he pointed the blowpipe to his chest and told me to blow hard down the hole. He told me to kill him. It was a joke. He laughed, I laughed, my sister laughed, my mother laughed.

I blew; he died. There was a poison arrow in the blowpipe. It contained curare. He died within minutes. Curare is the poison of the Indians. A blowpipe, if used with *superbes poumons*, can carry for at least sixty meters.

It took one hundred-thousandth of a gram to kill him.

The child comes forward, puts a paw out, says: 'Put her there, partner!'

Of course, I reciprocated the handshake. I put her there and, unintentionally, rhymed with my following sentence: 'Where is my chair?'

There was no answer. The child decides to whinny like a horse and gallop around my hut. I am furious.

I probably should've said this: the office isn't an office, it's a hut and the hut isn't really a hut.

It's a pharmacy. What year is it?

The child has an answer to everything, of course: 'It's

1865 and this is a pharmacy out on the frontiers of the Old West.'

You can't deny it: the child is pretty damned clever. My children have slush for brains and their genitals have not – and never will – form properly.

Not that this aggrieves me.

Gottfried – can I call him pops? Ah, old Pops! – specialised in curatives and poisons. His livelihood was a life and death.

He specialised in contradictions. He would often say he loved me. He would – equally – state that he hated me, too.

Gottfried was a terrible role model. I believe I have a part of him in my very soul.

And now, my only respite in this godforsaken hut – this cabin, this office, this place on the edge of nowhere – my chair, my precious spine-soothing chair, has been replaced by a five-year-old genius.

The child really knows how to get to me. He says: 'You've got a wife and two children?'

'Yes'.

'And she bothers you?'

'Yes'

'Your children. They're afflicted?'

'Yes'.

'With club foot and progeria?'

'Yes'.

The child is correct. One of my children has progeria. My little boy, Nat. He has a bulbous head riddled with veins. He looks like a very serious onion.

The child speaks clearly. His voice sounds like a soothing water, soaking my innards. My wife, in comparison, sounds like a foghorn.

Pops! He had a wife, too. She was a big-boned Bertha of a woman who rarely shaved her pits and shins and had nipples the size of marshmallows. Her lips were always liver-purple, face pale – drained – and constantly pensive.

She was my mother. Her name was Schwarzkopf Schwarzkopf.

She was addicted to opium. A Chinese man – tall and

thin and sallow – used to provide her with 60 grams of opium tincture by forging prescriptions for her. She died, too, in time, as we all must.

She died with her Dajensthen cradled in her arms. Her massive left nipple was lactating.

Good opium contains at least ten percent morphine, experts say. Mother's had zero.

The child sits down on the counter, wiping away the dust, telling me he was as American as they come. I said I am too, but the child seemed to guffaw, suggesting he thought I was telling a porky.

I believe this child is an angel. Or, at least, a cherub in disguise.

Cherub with a pipe.

And the child, it reminds me of my wife and her behaviour:

'I saw your wife galumph out from Glaser's saloon, gigantic with gin, wearing not a shred of decent cloth 'pon her shithouse frame.'

Of course, my face goes turnip and I am ashamed and wonder and wonder why my wife acts the way she does, why she persists in carrying out such rambunctious rituals.

'Child, what shall I do?'

My mother's name translates, roughly, to:

Black head, Black head.

Of course, I ask questions and it does not answer. When you need help the most, help is often preoccupied with the cooking, Gottfried used to tell me.

You need to be careful in a town like this. The sheriff is a reprobate. He has his eye on me. But I know things about his son.

Even saw his son climb out from the well only last week. He emerged and was soaked through, wearing what seemed to be women's face powder and panties. And the citizens. Is it enough to tell you my pharmacy – home to some of the world's deadliest poisons and curios – is the most popular place to shop in town?

The women, I find, mostly shop for arsenic. Why, even Old Hilly, Old Martha, Old Sally, Old Jane, Old Mary, Old Edith: even they seem to have new husbands now. In their gardens, I spy earthly rectangles of about six foot x two foot tattooing God's green grass.

The child says I'm weary. He says my hair dropped out because I am sad. He says I cannot muster up an erection because I am sad. He says I look like I have jaundice because I have jaundice.

Of course, he's not wrong. I ask the child again: what oh what oh what oh what shall I do about my wife?

And what of the children? The child mentions potassium cyanide, jokingly.

Gottfried, knowledgeable in all poisons, told me Countess Mathilde Chorinsky was killed using cyanide in Munich, 1867.

Her room had been prepared beforehand to accommodate a chum for high tea. The hotel employees burst into the room and found cakes and tea, untouched.

I tell the child: it's getting late.

The child is rosy cheeked and looking happy. As happy as I can remember anybody looking in my entire life. And he tells me of the ten inmates – invalids – who died in Jitschin, after being gassed. All an accident, of course.

The authorities were meant to gas out the insects, see. And the Spanish were good at this. Even had a guild called *fumigadores* that specialised in this. They were a guild of gassers.

In Jitschin, they not only killed the insects, but they killed all ten invalids, too. They were found by the authorities. The invalids' heads were slumped into their chests. They looked like they were asleep. Like chubby youths, rolls of fat reeling off beneath their chins.

The child bids me farewell: 'Farewell, farewell!'

I'll never forget the advice the child imparted to me. About my wife and children. I needed to ask some questions about myself, too. Where's the money going to come from after November? S'cold out, now. Need to wrap up. I rush home. To fix the family crisis. *Legumes! I shall cook legumes!*

I walk home past scraggy acres, hands incubated inside my jacket pockets. The rain, it starts. It keeps going. My legs walk across this alluvial land, the rainwater whoring itself upon the ground.

I see a man, old and unwise, crab walk to his outside clutching a scabbard. I think of my lout of a wife and my two children.

I dance all the way home to fix the problems in my life with glee and gusto and make a mental reminder to thank that chair for all it's done for me.

TORTOISE

1. The world's oldest tortoise was called Tu'i Malila.
2. Captain James Cook gifted Tu'i Malila to the royal family of Tonga in July 1777.
3. The year the Marquis de Sade was arrested and imprisoned in the Vincennes Fortress.
4. Also marked the death of Button Gwinnett.
5. Consider:
   Malcolm X was 39 years old when he was assassinated.
6. Captain James Cook was 50 years old when Hawaiian natives murdered him.
7. My grandmother died when she was 83.
8. Consider the 'immature' polyp.
9. My first cat died when she was ten.

10. Tu'i Malila died aged 188, which is older than all of the aforementioned subjects.

OLD

1. He combed his hair, saw his scalp. Not in a house. In a restaurant toilet.
2. A fear began to envelop his body. I'm old, he thought.
3. The white of his eye was now actually a dull straw colour, like somebody had urinated in them.
4. Just below the eyeball there was a black bag that resembled a fig.
5. His teeth had separated. In his youth, he was complimented for his fine teeth.
6. You could place a toothpick between each tooth; room to move.
7. He took his clothes off and observed his nipples.
8. Stay or leave? An indecision that went back to

childhood made itself present here in the toilet.

9. His eyes filled with tears and he balled up his fists.
10. Looking over at the exit door, he thought of his father's bald patch; how the sun caught it in such a way that it looked like its own little sun.

WEIGHT

1. Born by Cesarean section.
2. Unconsciously yearning for a traditional birth of passing through a vagina?
3. The inability to count, laughed at by children.
4. Remarkably good at cutting out shapes, however.
5. Leaving home:
   similar to a Cesarean section, he says.
6. Started at ten lbs; a fat toddler; a skinny teenager; middling in his twenties; alcoholic in his thirties.
7. Recurring dream:
   a mountain made of glass, fingers made of glass too.
8. The women in his life:
   mother / Martha / Mildred / Madeline / Melissa

/ Margaret.
9. The houses he lived in:
   bungalow / apartment / street / Harlem squat /
   Brownstone / tent.
10. Ended life an indeterminate weight.

PARKS

1. The boy chased by herons by the faux Swiss chalet.
2. The laughter of the elderly. The crumbs in the creases of their trousers.
3. The creases of their trousers like hills. Pushing my face into their crotch.
4. Grass only covers forty percent of the park. The rest is considered a 'recreation area.'
5. The jungle gym, knotted with children.
6. White children, black children, red children, yellow children.
7. The ducks that seemingly belong to the elderly are, in fact, adulterous.
8. The ducks move to another group of people, to get their bread elsewhere.

9. The children in the jungle gym; the elderly on the benches.
10. Each bench a memorial to somebody older than the elderly.

PAINTER

1. Ge Xiaoguang is now the official 'author' of Mao Zedong's portrait at Tiananmen Gate.
2. There have been others before him. There will be others after him.
3. Due to weather conditions and pollution, Ge Xiaoguang must repaint this portrait.
4. Other portraits used to hang in the square, but not anymore.
5. Ge Xiaoguang knows the face of Mao better than he knows himself.
6. When you look at light too long and afterwards, the light burns inside your own inner darkness.
7. Does Mao burn inside Ge Xiaoguang's inner darkness?

8. Ge Xiaoguang insists the face changes: he likens the act of repainting like 'reopening a door on history'.
9. Think about the position of the painting, coordinating the painting with the atmosphere of Tiananmen Rostrum, the influence of light – in the square, in the mind.
10. Will it be painted forever?

POOCH

My relationship with my dog has declined.

The table is clean because I clean it every day. To the left of me, a pile of papers that need reading. To the right of me, a cold cup of coffee. In front of me, a computer screen turned off. In the screen, my blurred silhouette. I blink but the reflection does not blink back.

On the journey home, I take the underground train. The train rattles. I prefer the crowded trains. Sometimes I like to smell people's armpits. Other times, I press myself into the buttocks of other people. My crotch sits snugly inside the crack of strangers.

A malaise has come over my dog. Once a pooch of great dignity, it is now, unfortunately, a shadow of its former self. It lies in the basket. I pet its head. It does not lift its head to acknowledge me. I turn the dog over and expose its abdomen. The hair is sparse here. The skin is pink and occasionally pocked with dark melanomas. I see nipples. I judge the dog for its nipples. I turn the dog back around. I pet it again. I take some dog food in my hand and put it under the dog's nose. It doesn't respond. It may as well be dead.

Later on in the evening, I watch a documentary about processed foods and a thought comes to me: when did I stop calling my dog by its name – Bob – and start calling it 'It'?

The city, like my dog, is not what it used to be. In the past, you could say the city and I shared a common bond. It understood me. That's why people move to big cities – because they feel the city somehow understands them. Urban people understand their flaws and feel that a city will hold them. People fit into their grooves here. But now, the city is unresponsive.

I wander the city after work, absentmindedly, and try to find this common bond again. I go out to the eastern fringes of the city to an elevated walkway above a road that leads out of the city. The metal railings are wet with condensation and shake with the thrum of cars driving into the darkness of out there. I hold the railings and take out my genitals. I take my sack and heave it upwards in my hands and let it rest on the railings. The cold touch of the railings upon my sack. My testicles, warm from the double layers I wear, droop over the railing. The image that comes to mind is that of an egg being broken over a dome, the yolk unsure whether it is running this way or that. The railing shakes and arouses me.

Later that night, I go into the centre of the city. I find myself in the red light district. I find an alleyway behind a bar. The gutters smell of urine and disinfectant. The walls in this alleyway are tiled and I begin to lick the tiles. I run my tongue all across the tiles, tasting and feeling the textures of this city. I find a discarded brick and notice it is a brick that 'typifies this great city'. During the nineteenth century, many of the bricks of this city became sooty and black in appearance. This particular brick is softer than a usual brick. I take the brick and bite into it. Although there is a risk this brick will damage my oesophageal lining, it is a risk worth taking. I feel that the distance between the city and I is shorter, that my physical engagement with my surroundings has opened up a new side to me. I feel that the city and I know each other intimately.

I go back home for the weekend. I have not seen my parents in over a year. Other family members are there. For example, my two sisters. My uncles and aunts, my nieces and nephews, my grandmothers and grandfathers, friends of the family. We are all gathered around a long dining table inside a modern conservatory. On the side, there are a number of potted plants.

We eat dinner and I attempt to bond with my family. But as they look at me, they form a judgment. They are not city folk. They know what I am. They do not think about me, here, present in this house but instead they think of the 'me' back in the city, like a ghostly double of who I am.

When I was young, my father read me bedtime stories. But I never listened to him, instead focusing on his neck, his ears and hands. I often wondered, as a child, if my hands would be as thick as my fathers.

In the present day, I now realise my father's hands are not thick. Perhaps they have lost their thickness, over time. Perhaps they were never thick in the first place.

As we eat dinner, I lick my two front teeth. A sudden dislocation occurs in my mind. I become self-conscious about my mouth, its movements, my teeth, all of them rooted into my skull. I put my knife and fork down and do not eat another bite of food. The licking of my teeth, reminding me of skulls, also reminded me that I was mortal.

Upon returning home, I realise I had left the dog alone in the house. The dog is dead. I turn it over and rub its stomach in a circular motion.

In what could be construed as 'coincidence', I see one of my friends post a picture of two basset hounds lying by an oven. A friend of my friend comments: Oh you're kidding me? You have basset hounds? He then posts two framed pictures of two more basset hounds and says: Our boys... Sadly not with us anymore... Henry and Hecter.

The spelling of Hecter, perhaps, should be Hector.

I bury my dog out in a park, late on a Sunday night. I do it in the middle of a football pitch.

As I go to work on Monday, I think about dogs, the city and me. I think of the comment I read – Sadly not with us anymore – and try to work a meaning into this sentence but I cannot.

A SIMPLE FACT

In the same way my mother and father, my two sisters and various friends were dying or had died of cancers, I was dying of life.

I was dying so hard of life, I could barely breathe. My ears and nose and eyes were sick to their stomach of life. My toes curled at the thought of the word *continue*.

"Take me, death!" I screamed at the microwave. "Take me now!"

What was there left in this life? Life, I said to my child, is a real stinker.

It was all my husband. His name is Ismael. We married when we were young, straight out of school and didn't bother pursuing our interests in life. He wanted children, I wanted to write. But no, he said, let's do it my way. So I did.

He'd wake up in the middle of the night, sweating, and grab me by the shoulders and say: "Baby! Honey pie and light of my life, I want to stick a kid in you. I want a bit of me and a bit of you to come out of your vagina and I want to raise it. And then maybe a few more pups. What do you say?"

Our flesh was taut and his sperm was alive and my eggs were ready, so we did it. We had a night of passionless sex. We didn't know how. What book were we supposed to have read? We'd heard of moves and legs intertwined, but how were we to know how to do these things?

"Aren't you supposed to kiss me?" I said.

"But now? I'm in you. I can't kiss and be in you!"

And maybe he was right, I thought. Can one lock tongues and be genital-locked too?

I remember looking at the clock.

Ismael did too, sweat forming on his meaty brow.

Time was running out. The moment was perfect, he said. He was indeed in me and I guess I'd lost that battle, but there you go. He didn't give it any gusto, let's put it that way, and after a few minutes, I was filled with the liquid of an average man with no care in the world for my body but to be a vessel to help him live forever.

I spent nine months with a child inside of me, going from the size of a pea to the size of a baby, and I would like to add I was especially pleased when it left me. The baby girl was born and Ismael named it after his grandmother, Eliza.

"Look at her," he exclaimed. "She looks just like her grandmother."

He was of course wrong because Eliza looked the same way all babies did, which is like nothing at all.

And it was more worrying that his grandmother was six months dead at this point and I wanted to prove a point to him that his grandmother didn't look any good at all anymore, that perhaps she had bugs for eyes, worms for veins and a meaty football head with leprous hairs sprouting out of it. I wish I would've said this!

I pushed my child around parks in a dramatic pram. I met other women who were all similarly impregnated by ambitious men who had more interest in money than spending more time with us.

"Now I've pushed one pup out," I said, "Ismael doesn't even look at me the same anymore."

The other women laughed. They cackled and had bony arms and knees. They were all edges and lipstick. Their faces were televisions showing white noise. They were dishwater dull ladies, all there in the park, laughing and laughing through their dumb maws.

"You need to try some tricks to keep your man," said Joan Crocker. I didn't bother asking *what* tricks and I think at that time they continued to speak, but I tuned out.

I thought of my husband as a dog on its hind legs, a small novelty collar around his neck as I, ten feet tall, dangled a treat over his mouth.

But there was a simple fact here: I was a woman who had been cast out. My husband, my *pumpkin pie*, he'd deserted me. I was alone in the house, growing older and accustomed to sofas and ottomans.

I grew bored with my daily routine and got a job. This, too, was boring. I remember waking up one morning and realised my job was four walls, a floor and a ceiling. I screamed at my job and shook it like a hooligan. "How dare you eat my time!"

It was true, my job was fat and greedy and ate my time all up. I was a surprised, then, that one morning I woke up and my job had disappeared. Where did it go? For the life of me, I don't know. But it had gone and I didn't question this, and it was back to the boredom of home instead, feeding Eliza and staring at my own naked body in mirrors at different angles.

So instead, every day, I would stalk different men. There I was, strolling down the avenues of this great city, past the homeless with the spittle in the corners of their crack-starved mouths, past the legless hobos and business men and women, past the hotdog sellers and door men, past grates and trash and I'd pick a man.

One day, I picked what I'd like to call a beanpole. I thought, what's his name? I called him Frederick. He sat down at first and sipped on a plastic cup of coffee. I observed his knuckles, white and bony. His skin too. The word mottled came to mind, though I wasn't quite sure if that was right. He folded his legs, so far in fact, that I wondered if his testicles had *one-potato-two-potatoed* each other.

Eliza was in the pram getting older by the second. She cried a little, but for the most part she was silent. In her, I saw my husband, which was a great disappointment.

I used my daughter, my own flesh and blood, as armour against the city more than anything.

The city was a terrifying place. The buildings reached into the sky like beggars' hands, I thought. When I was following Frederick, I didn't look so much at him, but at everybody around him. How many eyeballs were in this one mile radius? If I plucked every eyeball out of their heads, what size would the vat be, if I chose to put them in a vat that is. And then I thought of genitalia. I thought if I removed every penis from every man, how long would that road stretch on for? I thought of mountains made of breast, surrounding the city.

Frederick moved through the city as if he knew he were being followed by a woman. He went into impressive places and struck impressive poses. He knelt down on his haunches and I saw his sinewy ankles.

What feelings did this stoke in me? I wasn't sure. Eliza was so quiet that she may well have been dead, so I wet my finger and put it under her nose. Alive.

But Frederick moved on. He weaved through the city, down alleyways and into hotel foyers. I waited for him. I read newspapers and thought of cutting holes into them, being what I thought a real spy was. I spent some time looking at my hands and thinking how old they were now and how my husband remarked on the lack of tautness in my skin. He would pinch the skin on my arms and stretch it out. He'd pinch my sides. I really was a sucker, I thought, there in the foyer of an expensive hotel.

How I'd love to slowly murder my husband for planting his seed in me. How would he like it? If I planted something in him. He would cry. He'd cry like a little baby.

The day waned. Frederick had spent many hours walking, so much so that there was a giant boogie-board-sized sweat patch on his back. He was a perspiring man. I had known perspiring men in my life and, when I saw his sweat patch, had weirdly regretted not recording this list of perspiring men in a notebook somewhere.

I wondered what his flanks felt like. Suddenly I felt the need to touch everything in the city, to pluck those eyeballs out and hold Frederick like a new born. I felt like submerging him in a deep, dark water.

The moon was out and cast the city in a white glow. Frederick had wandered into the park in the centre of the city. It was open all hours. The stories I'd heard about young ladies wandering in here alone, about men preying in the bushes.

Had I seen my husband recently? Had Ismael come

home one night this week or the week before? I couldn't remember. He was a ghost who drifted in and out of my life, pinching my flesh and stretching my skin in cruel and humiliating ways.

But there was Frederick in the dark, his clothes falling from him like rotting skin. I peered into the dark, Eliza just in front of me. He was moving down into a lake and I saw bumps all over his body. He seemed to be getting larger and perhaps spouting gills. Had I seen this right? I didn't know. I didn't at all. I also didn't care much for the safety of my own home and all its conveniences. I pushed Eliza to the side and said I would be gone indefinitely.

I slipped my shoes off and followed Frederick into the lake and I felt my body all over, feeling gills of my own. The lake was dark, but I knew I could breathe down there now.

CATS

He divided his cat in two with a butter knife. This was how bored he was, how dissatisfied he was with city life. The cat, lying atop a dining room table with a plastic red and white-checkered sheet, had two glassy eyes. He buried half the cat in a small memorial garden around the corner from his apartment. He buried the other half under his floorboards. He was still bored. He thought about putting the cat back together again, going backwards through its life and then going forwards again.

ITEMS

A great man began to drop things. *He used to be able to hold the crockery*, his colleagues said. They still revered him and respected him. *He has really nice hair*, said one student. *It's grey but not stringy*. Other people on the campus congratulated him on his kind nature and ability to pick up shy woodland creatures. His thinking, his reasoning, it's unparalleled. But then, one day in the staff room, he began to drop everyday objects. His hands would go stiff, fingers stretched out and he would drop cups, plates, forks and knives. He would move to the other side of the room and stay in a corner. The younger staff members began to make a note of all the things he dropped: teapot, duck figurine, satchel, watch, pen, pencil, protractor, pile of books, tumbler, chair, duck figurine, wig.

HOLE IN THE HEAD

I woke up in the streets again. It was becoming a common occurrence for me, blacking out and waking up in trash, in doorways, in rooms I didn't know. I'd been doing this for what seemed like months now. I did terrible things with my friends. We were marauders. We kept secrets between us.

I felt my head and looked at my hands. Blood. This was, I believed, a normal thing but as I tipped my head forward, it poured out like cranberry juice into my hands.

Wow, I said.

I stood up, unsteady from a night of drinking what felt like hot tar in my stomach, and stumbled over to the nearest person.

Hey you, I said. Looky here. I pointed at my head. What do you see?

You've got a hole in your head, the person said.

I should say this person was in fact a lady, and a fine lady at that. She wore a bonnet and a large dress that concealed several giggling children and there they peeked at me and pointed and filled me with shame.

Thank you, madam, I said, and curtsied. The blood sloshed around like the sea in a tempest and splashed out over her large child-hiding dress. Apologies, I said as I righted myself, pretending my spine was a pole in the ground and walked off stiff-like, trying not to spill any more of my blood anywhere.

I walked the city carefully thinking of what to do. I wasn't near any mirrors so I couldn't judge how big the hole was and I was hungry too. Food, I thought, let me eat food. I followed my stomach through the twisty streets of the city, past the beggars with their strawberry noses, their pissed-on shirts and called them dropsy-legged bitches, kicked dirt in their faces. I didn't care. I had a hole in my head, so I could do what I wanted.

I came upon a café and waltzed in, a-one-and-a-two-and-a-one and I was clicking my fingers in time to the sound in my head, the sound of skull and brain and blood beating and pulsing.

I pirouetted over to the bar and slammed my hand on it. Good sir! What sandwiches do you have?

All sorts. Tell me what you'd like.

Cheese! Lettuce! And a gherkin. Do you sell gherkins? And gin?

Yes.

I slammed my money down and a bit of blood spilled over. Bring it to my table, I screamed.

And I went over and sat down with my gin in hand and saw my two dirty rotten friends. I wondered if we'd agreed to meet here or if it was just chance.

Good morning Toby and Jonesy, how the devil are you?

They were two pig-faced fellows, yes, but friends, *good friends*, and we had made a pact long ago to keep each other's secrets. I knew, for example, that Toby once buggered Jonesy when he was drunk and planted his seed in his anal cavity. Jonsey, too, had murdered a child and stole a bottle of milk from it. But what did they know about me?

Bloody hell, what have you done to your head Mister Peacock?

I don't know. I have a hole in it, though.

Well that's quite clear, yes, yes, yes, said Jonsey. He was drinking milk. Silly Jonsey and his obsession with milk...

Can we hide some bad thoughts in there, Mister Peacock?

I said I don't see why not. I tilted my head and let Jonsey put a few bad thoughts in the hole.

You promise you won't say anything about any of that, right Peacock?

Cross my heart.

And how about me? I've got a few things that, uh, need concealing, said Toby.

Toby, pop them in, but please – *please* – can you check how much room is in there?

He dipped a finger in my head and peered in.

Looks pretty roomy in there. I've got a sexual perversion for a married woman that would fit quite snugly by your brain.

Then pop 'er in!

And he did. By the end of the morning, my hole was filled with the perversions and crimes and secrets of my two pig-faced chums and it weighed on me terribly.

I'd eaten my sandwich by this point and had several gins, so I stood up, wobbled slightly and held my head with both hands. It felt like it was about to fall off and break. A tiny piece of Jonsey's buggering had lodged itself behind my eye, but I didn't mind.

The weight, however, was unbelievable. What else had they put in there?

I asked them and they both said nothing, nothing that they hadn't told me already.

Well okay then, I said. I have no other choice but to believe you...

But there were some images in my hole that were unfamiliar, that didn't sound like anything I'd agreed to store for Jonsey and Toby.

There was a pause. A long silence. And then there were goodbyes and handshakes, kisses on the cheek, Toby's buttocks, a head, a sword, ducks and ponds, flickering past my eyes.

As I left, they waved me off, grinning and laughing at me and I wondered if they were perhaps in on a big joke I didn't know about.

SOFT FRUIT IN THE SUN

The shape of my back fit Terrence's perfectly. Two smaller men threaded us together with wire and thick needles and my legs dangled down his back as we were tightened closer.

I looked like a meat backpack.

Oh, the places I'll show you, he said. Terrence clapped and jigged as we bled on the floor.

Do you remember when we met, my darling? He asked this to me as if I didn't already know.

I do, I said. Ten years ago. I was young and hadn't seen

the world. *You don't know culture*, he'd told me that night. *Here, look at this*, and there in the palm of his hand was a small scrap of culture he had taken from his pocket. *Take it, study it.*

I did. I studied it and I could feel myself becoming a better person.

Wow, I told him the next day over the phone, *thank you. Thank you from the bottom of my heart.*

Come round to my house, he said. *I have a bookshelf with many books. You can read them all with me. I have a beautiful lilting voice.*

So I went over. Terrence sat me on his lap and he read books to me. Pathology, agriculture, stories old and new. He read with a big booming voice, the voice of a confident, educated man.

Here, look, he said. *This is James Joyce. Eat it.* He tore out a page from the book and I ate it.

Thanks so much! I said.

We courted. He took me to see theatre and operas. I didn't understand the fuss. He bought expensive drinks and I swallowed them. We had sex and with each passing year, our genitals grew softer like fruit in the sun.

In many ways, being on his back was the only way our relationship could go.

We didn't speak much in the first two days. *Teething problems*, he muttered to himself.

I ached and moaned a lot. *How do I go to the toilet?*, I asked. Terrence didn't know. Then he did know. *Just piss down my back. And if you're going to drop a deuce, drop it, but do it quickly.*

We learnt how to live this way. In the day, as he walked, I also saw the world from his back's point of view. I saw people recede, buildings recede. I saw walls and bricks and dead ends.

Can we go to a different country?, I asked. *I've seen everything from the front and the back here.*

Of course, Terrence said. *Perhaps the view will be different for you.*

So he went online and booked a flight. *Tap tap tap*, I could hear his fingers. I asked which country and he said nothing. I guessed it was a surprise.

Air travel made us bleed a lot more than usual, so we used the vomit bags to pool it all. We took up an entire aisle.

Sorry, I said, to various people who needed the leg room. *I'm so sorry*. An elderly woman with two elephantine legs glared at me. I didn't know what to do but figured I would be okay on Terrence's back.

We arrived in a different country. I didn't know which country it was, but Terrence walked around for hours so as to give me a view.

Wow, I said. *This is special. To see things recede in a different country. To be on a man's back in a different country.*

He showed me different places and swivelled around to give me a full view. I didn't understand the beauty of it all the time, but I feigned interest.

What did we do next? We couldn't figure it out. Something was wrong.

You bore me, he said.

But I love you. I didn't. I had agreed to be on his back, yes. But I didn't understand why I'd agreed to this.

Yes, I know. But you're from a poor family. Your father has smudged skin and your mother only knows potatoes.

I was silent, on his back.

It doesn't matter if you're holding my hands, on my lap or sewn to my back. There's no teaching some people. You are unsalvageable.

The next day we found two people to unthread us. It took a long time and we bled everywhere again. But it was done. We walked off in opposite directions and did not look back at each other. We kept moving forwards. Maybe Terrence kept walking forwards until he died. I planned to. I had forgotten what Terrence looked like and everything I looked at was without meaning and made me sick, which was perhaps a lesson learned.

SWALLOWING

— an essay

I was 12 when I choked on a small piece of bread. It is difficult to say exactly when I choked: I don't remember the day or the month, but only that I was 12 and that it was white bread and that, when it happened, I ran into the kitchen and told my mother that it was stuck in my throat. She said I should drink some water. She said the water would wash it away.

But the water did nothing. In fact, the small morsel of bread grew larger and larger over the course of that evening. Years later, my mother told me over the phone that she has always regretted giving me that piece of bread.

She actually said: *I curse the day I gave you that bread.*

We went to visit my grandmother's house that night. I remember the carpet in the hallway: it was covered in dog hair.

Many years later, after my grandmother had died of dementia, I had a morbid thought: that the dog had now inherited the house and that the dog had lived longer, in dog years, than my grandmother. And then I thought: when the dog was dead, the dog hair would outlive the dog; at least until another person moved in and tore out that carpet and made the house their own.

But when I was 12, I focused on the carpet. My mind needed something to focus on. I ran up and down that carpet and said I was choking. I said that the bread was growing inside my throat. My mother, naturally, thought nothing of this. I had always been seen as neurotic. This probably started when I was nine years old. I had developed a nervous twitch of the arm: it would flex it quickly, like a bodybuilder showing his biceps to an audience. My mouth would open to yawn and I could hear my jaw crack. I still do this when I am nervous. I feel like my muscles are constantly at work, twitching and moving. I feel charged with electricity. A phrase I often say now is that my nerves are *jangled.*

But when I was 12 years old: a week had passed and the bread had grown even bigger in my throat. I remember thinking that the bread completely blocked my throat, that there was no way any food could ever fit down my throat again. I would put my fingers over my Adam's apple and feel around, thinking that I could actually feel the bread.

And then I stopped. I stopped eating solids. I did not eat a proper solid food until I was 18 years old.

*

I live in a warehouse conversion in Hackney. It won't be there for long as it is planned for demolition soon to make way for expensive flats.

This is the view from my window:

The room is small and convenient. It is cheap and I pay cash in hand to a landlord who runs a factory downstairs. Chinese people sew clothes for 12 hours a day and have faces like leather bags.

My view overlooks a car parts graveyard, a place where cars are stripped, where axels, calipers, windshields, exhausts, steering wheels and leather chairs lay strewn about the concrete surface.

Even here in the middle of busy Hackney, there is a kind of solitude, a small warehouse room where I feel myself turning ever inwards, thinking daily about my throat and swallowing.

*

I have always had a problem with swallowing. I see swallowing similar to the way I used to step onto the escalator as a child: with fear and trepidation, I went to put my foot on the moving steps, but didn't, always about to, but aborting the movement until I had to take a leap of faith and just do it.

I was and still am conscious of the beating of my heart. I can see myself as a child about to take that leap of faith and can hear the fluttering of breath. It echoes through the years. I make the same fluttering now as I chew my food and make the leap of faith to swallow the food. Even now at 28, I can't swallow food without a drink of water by my side. If I drink alcohol, the fear of swallowing is lessened considerably but I try not to drink anymore due to my temper.

The anger started just after I swallowed the bread. At school, I was often reprimanded by the head of the year for hitting people. Sometimes I threw chairs around. I threatened to hurt people. I tried to prove I was strong by punching metal poles with my knuckles. My knuckles would bleed or would be reddened by the impact of bone and metal. I can hear the sound now of my bone hitting the metal and I think of the anger as frustration, a frustration born from the fact that whilst other people my age were healthy, I wasn't.

I was a runner at school, a sprinter. I used to run the 100m, 200m and took part in the relay race too. Although this may not have meant much to anybody else – it was after all, just school – it meant a lot to me. I had something I was good at. I thought perhaps in the future this is something I could do well at. But as the years went on, I couldn't keep up. At 13, I was one of the fastest in my school and locally. As I became thinner, I became weaker. My heart couldn't take it. My legs couldn't do it. And there lay a source of frustration: not being able to keep up.

Lost time.

The only way to articulate my frustration was through violence. Even the films I watched were violent: Japanese films like *Ichi the Killer*, Abel Ferrara's *Driller Killer* and countless zombie films. I never watched the films for their story. Instead, I would rewind and play the goriest moments, the moments where bodies were ripped apart; the moment the drill goes into the temple.

It was as if I felt I didn't have time to consume an entire narrative. I had to consume only the essentials: the gore, the money shots, the one-liners. In many ways, my eating disorder not only frustrated me but also made me incapable of consuming literature or cinema or music in a traditional way. There were no beginnings, middles or ends: I started wherever I wanted. I moved through the narrative like I was convulsing: forward-winding and rewinding, forward-winding, rewinding, pausing and focusing on fragments. Becoming fixated on paused faces and locations, houses and the trinkets in the background; noticing things that had no bearing on the plot but felt like a secret knowledge, access to a world I had control over.

In Woody Allen's *Hannah and her Sisters* (1986) – a film I can no longer watch – I didn't watch for the narrative: I was looking at the character's bookshelf. And there, in the middle of the story, in the middle of a dramatic dialogue, I found and still find myself looking at a copy of *Loon Lake* by E.L. Doctorow sitting on a shelf, waiting to be seen, waiting to be known, waiting for me to consume it.

With books, I wanted knowledge, but I was too impatient to read the entire thing. I was too tired to read the books, too, with my stomach growling and, often, large ulcers the size of peas on my lower lip. I often imagined eating the pages of the books in order to consume the knowledge faster, an image that has stuck with me ever since. Instead of truly understanding a book on the pathology of mental diseases, I thought of tearing out a page – perhaps a list of plates showing *haematoma auris* – with the illustrations so alien to me, their colour and potential so great, and then swallowing it whole.

*

It is difficult to mention dates.

It is difficult to mention specific events that mark this journey between the ages of 12 to 18. In many ways it seemed like a fever or, perhaps, an hallucination.

Reading a book review by Ginia Bellafante in the *New York Times*, 2008:

> *Mollie Fancher is never mentioned in* Going Hungry, *a collection of first-person essays on the allure of dangerously austere eating, but she is a paradigm for a view in which anorexia emerges less palpably as a humiliating physical and psychological affliction than as an elevated state of mind, an intellectualised hallucination.*

It was a space in my life that I lost. I see it as lost time.

And looking back on it, yes, it does seem like a kind of elevated state of mind, a kind of intellectualised hallucination. And although it is difficult to organise my thoughts in regards to this lost time, there are fragments that come back to me, little pulses from the past that throb in my mind and remind me of the things I have tried to bury.

I often wonder how people write about themselves with such accuracy. People who write about dates or describe exactly what their family was wearing that day. People who write about the weather and then, in quotations, write down exactly what their brother or sister said.

It is what people call 'creative non-fiction'. Memoir only means a written record, an account of a life. This doesn't always necessarily mean the truth, of course. The accuracy I write of is there to colour the truth so it is more interesting, perhaps. Or to provide a presence where, in reality, there is an absence. To fill in that *lost time* I spoke about to provide a narrative structure to hold on to.

But this will not do.

In my mind, those years from 12 to 18 are truly marked by absence. And in the place of absence there is truly fiction.

This is where you disappear when you are haunted by reality. Fiction is, at least to me, a coping technique.

It takes my mind off the images of my thin body, off the physical humiliation of those days, off swallowing, off choking, off feeling too close to my body. Fiction is alive. It provided the presence to my absence; kept me going when I thought I could no longer cope anymore.

*

The obsession that there was something in my throat. Reading about things people have swallowed, objects that were actually there. A boy aged four with a pair of toy opera glasses in his oesophagus.

But then there is the idea of something there that is not. In Don DeLillo's *Libra* (1988), Jack Ruby tells one of his dancers about his mother:

> *My mother, this is the God's honest truth, I swear to God, she spent thirty years of her life claiming there was a fishbone stuck in her throat. We listened to her constantly.*

Doctors, clinics, they searched for years with i n s t r u m e n t s. Finally she had an operation. There was nothing caught in her throat, absolutely, guaranteed. She comes home from the hospital. The fishbone is there.

I am Jack Ruby's mother.

The thought that there is something there, that there was a foreign object in my throat. It is June 6th, 2016, and I note down in my journal that I should research this, perhaps talk to others who have or have had eating disorders because of a fear of a foreign object in their throat.

*

I have never been good at swallowing. I can't take pills. Even with a simple paracetamol, I still need to chew it in half, or sometimes chew it completely, in order to swallow it. I refuse to eat fresh fish or cooked salmon fillets. If I do, by some twist of fate, do end up with salmon on my plate, I usually dissect the fish, trying to pick out the bones, much to everybody's chagrin.

I was once at dinner with some colleagues and somebody saw me picking bones from the salmon. She said, *Even I taught my child to mush his fish up with the fork.* She suggested, then, that I did not know the obvious thing to do in this situation, this trick that everybody knew about except me. She suggested, I thought, that my education in how to approach food was lacking. And perhaps she was right. I don't think I do have a very good history of chewing and swallowing food, or a good relationship with it for that matter.

I think back to a time when I was perhaps four or five years old. I can't quite remember what the situation is, but I am sitting on the floor next to a Chesterfield sofa and my mother is holding a plate of food in front of me. She twirls a fork around the spaghetti and then puts it in her mouth. She chews the food into mulch and then puts it back on the fork. She feeds it back to me. I eat what my mother has chewed.

My mother chewed my food for me, like a bird. This is called premastication. Although I believe that my mother did this with the best intentions, I also believe that it had an effect on me. In the act of chewing for me, my mother had already done half the action. There was no need for my jaw to learn that movement.

This translated into other parts of my life. We only ever had a bath up until our third house when I was 18, so when I was young I sat in the bath and let my mother wash my hair for me. I didn't like the water going in my eyes and couldn't be bothered to reach for a towel so my mother handed me one. She was my mother, yes, but also an extension of me.

*

With food, however, I think maybe my problems go back to this point, the point of premastication. Following that, it seemed I started to develop a heightened sense of my own body.

I was a vociferous reader and read anything that was lying around the house. Our bookshelves were often filled with pathology books that my mother had taken from work. I still read them to this day. I am still fascinated by the words in these books, the pictures, the cross sections and case studies of people whose bodies, suddenly and without warning, wage war upon them.

*

Today is Monday 9th, 2016, 16 years since I swallowed that morsel of bread that grew bigger than I could ever imagine. I was on the phone to my mother earlier today. I asked her if she remembered that period of my life and she said yes. I find that difficult to believe. If anything, I have buried that moment, buried it very far into my mind and have, until now, believed that it was gone and that I was better. Now, for example, I weigh 10.7 stone, which is 67.94814 kg, which is 149.8 lbs. This is healthy and I believe that I am a healthy man of 28 years old.

But there are moments when I twitch. My ex-girlfriend, for example, said that I twitched when I read. I twitched when I concentrated on something. I also make odd facial stretches and rub my eyes constantly. I frown and clench my teeth in moments of calm. I flex my biceps repeatedly until they hurt and sometimes I stretch the tendons on my neck and give a strange grin to nothing in particular. I open my mouth wide like a yawn, but no sound comes out except the crunching of my jaw on both of its hinges. I can hear ear wax slop just above those hinges as I do it.

I am not in control of my body. These twitches seem like pulses or frequencies from another time in my past, lost signals from 16 years ago. I am not better, it seems. Recently I have had difficulty swallowing in front of others and have also found it difficult to swallow things without taking many breaths – similar to taking a leap of faith – before a solid can go down my throat. When I am invited to dinner, I drink. If I am in a café I usually eat with my back to everybody. I eat facing a wall. If anybody looks at me, I find I focus on chewing, focus on breathing and swallowing. Then I choke.

Recently, it seems that there are some troubling foods: the raw carrot, for example, still poses a threat to me. As do peanuts. I can swallow a peanut, but then it seems to explode in my throat like a grenade and I feel traces of it hours later lining my oesophagus.

When I was on the phone to my mother, I asked her what she thought of those six years.

She said: *It ruined my life.*

I pushed her for more detail and she said: *Yes, it ruined our life. A friend once told me that you are only as happy as your most unhappy child.*

*

There are questions to consider: Did I make my father's hair turn grey? Was I a contributing factor to my mother's hair loss? Did I or didn't I want to commit suicide? Would I have turned out differently had I not choked on a piece of bread? Why did I hide food down the backs of radiators? Why did I flush food down the toilet? Why did I think that my parents couldn't see me putting food into my pockets during meals? What would my sexual appetites be like if I hadn't starved myself for six years? Why am I obsessed with looking at emaciated bodies? Why do I twitch? Will I ever return to the house where I stopped eating? Do I get along with food? Does food get along with me?

And so on.

*

At 10am every day, I would cook a tomato soup on an Aga and stir it clockwise. Never anti-clockwise. If I did stir it anti-clockwise, I would have to spit in the bin three times.

If I were at school, I would visit the tuck shop and buy a cup of soup. It filled me up only temporarily. I would wait until 10pm in the evening to eat another soup at home.

And then there are parallels between the routine in my life and the routine I found in fiction. Take, for example Robert Bresson's *A Man Escaped*[1] (1956). I watched it during the height of my eating disorder on a small television in my room. It was a cheap VHS and I sat close to the screen to see it in all its detail. The television was a round-screened thing,

[1] Original title: *Un condamné à mort s'est échappé ou Le vent souffle où il veut*

the cathode ray tubes burning through my retinas.

I saw my eating disorder as a way of doing time.

There was an almost religious intensity to the day-to-day routines. If I did something that did not fit the routine, I would punish myself.

I found and still find comfort in prison movies. The prison movie was a good coping technique to get me through this stage in my life. I saw something in the routine of prison and the routine of my life. Of course, my prison was self-imposed. But sometimes I thought that I enjoyed my prison, that there was a comfort to being confined, a solitude and fuzziness to being ill.

Again, it reminds me of DeLilo's *Libra*, when Lee Harvey Oswald is talking to Dale Fitzke, 'a cripple':

> *What do you like best about the darkroom? It's the way my room used to look when I had a fever. Childhood fevers were the best times... Do you remember what it was like, being under the blankets, sweating, as a kid? A fever is a secret thing. It's like falling*

down a hole where no one
can follow but there's no
terror or pain because you
don't even feel like yourself.

The eating disorder as a contradiction: that it was a something I desperately wanted to be rid of, but also found comfort in. The comfort of the fever. The pain that does not even seem real because you don't even feel like yourself. The idea that the eating disorder is a heightened sense of intellectualism, that it is almost like a hallucination, a fever, a dream.

There are memories of being in my room, closing my door to everybody. Computer games, VHS tapes, DVDs, books.

There are memories of looking at pornography too, at naked women, breasts, vaginas, arms, legs, feet. These were the days before fast internet connections. These were the days when I would print off pornographic images on my computer and look at them. The images never printed properly sometimes due to a lack of ink or a shoddy printer. I saw women in fragments, in body parts. I fell in love with whatever image I had in front of me. Perhaps it was the torso of a pornography star, her legs removed by the printer. This was a problem back when my printer ran out of ink: I could never fully print the female form. Sometimes it was just the collarbone, strong and tanned and other times just a high-heeled shoe, a veiny foot and its anklet. I never saw the naked female form as one thing: I saw it in pieces. There, on a badly printed page, was what I thought a woman's body was.

*

I think in numbers. Eating at 10am and 10pm. 12 hours. The age I developed the eating disorder: 12. Coincidences. When you watch your weight on a scale every day, you think in numbers. How many stone, kilograms, pounds. At one point, six stone. Maybe less. I couldn't study mathematics, but I could study weight and pounds, stone and kilograms. Measurements of the body. Chest size in inches. Tape measures around my wrist and ankles, noting down fluctuations. Penis size in inches. Sometimes centimeters. Noting down growth on paper. Creating line graphs of subtle differences.

*

At dinnertime, my mother would sit at the table with my sister. My father rarely ate food with us because he was at work until late. So there we were, the rest of the family eating together. But I saw my mother and sister as two policewomen who were watching me constantly. Their eyes upon me. I put food in my mouth and chewed it. I chewed it and chewed it until it was mulch. I usually kept the mulch in the right cheek and then asked to be excused. I was allowed to go.

What else could they say? I think I used to see tears in my mother's eyes. My sister would just look at her plate and say nothing. When I got to the toilet I would place the food in my hand and carefully lower it into the toilet so as not to make a splash. There was a window above the toilet that could be opened and I could throw the food out of that. It is difficult to remember what kind of window it was: was it a sash window or the type that opened to the left with a latch?

This eventually had to stop because my father found the discarded food just below the window one evening. I don't remember what evening it was, but that does not matter. He found it, which is what matters. I threw the food out the window, which is what matters.

The house was a Georgian house and I remember this because I liked history. I learnt about how a Georgian door was different to a Victorian door, for example. I learnt how the style of a Georgian house was nicer than that of the far more ornate, gothic inclinations of the Victorian house.

I liked to run my fingers along the sandstone of our house. I like surfaces. In our living room there was a marble fireplace that I would run my fingers across every day as a matter of urgency. If there were any other marble objects or surface in that room or, in fact, any other room of the house, I would have to touch them too. Routines. Following routine. If I didn't follow the routines, perhaps something terrible would happen. Touching marble, stirring soup. Limiting a life to movements, to the feel of things.

I didn't just discard food down drains, toilets or throw it out windows. I would sometimes place the food down holes in the floor, too. In the upstairs bathroom, there was a boiler cupboard and just next to the boiler was a deep, dark hole where the pipes ran down underneath the floorboards. I would place the food down there and hope that my parents never found it. But it created this smell, similar to vomit, that I think my mother noticed but said nothing about.

*

Why did you do it?

My mother asked me this. We spoke about it the way we usually spoke about it: with pauses, breaks, sighs. There was no fluency to conversation when we spoke about this subject.

Why did you do it?

As if I had a choice. I don't remember the exact day or

the exact month when it started.

Lost time.

But who would willingly choose to put themselves through this? Going to bed and raising my arm above my head and holding my wrist to see how much room there was between finger and wrist. Checking if bodily functions were working.

Masturbating into aerosol caps.

The routine: clockwise, always clockwise.

Superstitions: if you see something bad, spit on the floor. If you step on a crack, spit on the floor. If you're in public and can't spit on the floor, spit into your sleeve. Sleeves dried with spittle, mucus. Lips constantly lined with ulcers. Going to bed starving. Crying myself to sleep. Punching walls with frustration. Holding knives to my wrists most weeks. Of course, some days these were sharp knives, other days these were butter knives. I was not educated in the ways of suicide yet at the age of 13 or 14.

And then I remember speaking to my sister about it, some years later. *What happened?*, she asked me. I don't know. It just happened.

Then there was a pause.

Always the pause.

Not knowing what to say.

And then she said: *Mum always wondered if you were abused.*

As in touched?

By somebody, maybe, yes.

I said I hadn't been abused but it placed an idea in my head that perhaps I had.

I don't remember the exact date or exact day that it happened.

Lost time.

Perhaps I had. Perhaps I thought I had been.

*

Sixteen years later, I spoke about my eating disorder with my mother. We spoke on the phone. It was Tuesday night at 20:38 and lasted for exactly one hour. I know this because it happened now. I remember things now because I want to remember them.

The first thing we spoke about was the fact that I was writing this book. I asked my mother if it was a good idea to write this and she said yes. I asked for permission, as if this disorder was not mine. She said it was mine and that it was a good idea to make something positive out of something so overwhelmingly negative.

Then I spoke about how I don't remember things so well from this period in my life and asked what she remembered.

She said: *I remember your face. You had a face that was hard as nails, but you were scared. You were a scared boy. And you were a teenage boy too, so I had to be careful with what I said, but you were scared.*

She said: *It was like you weren't there.*

I asked her why I couldn't remember things, why we never spoke about things when this all happened.

She said: *No words. There are no words. It was like walking through a fog.*

When she compared that time to walking through a fog, I am immediately reminded of the hallucinations, the fevers.

*

She said it was like it was all happening in slow motion.

And after she spoke about the fog, she said: *We weren't getting any better.* At first I found it strange that my mother combined us into one entity, but she was right: it wasn't just I who went through this, but it was my mother, my father and my two sisters too.

She said: *I couldn't see a future for both of us.* Again, combining our lives as one. This sentence is usually a sentence one reserves for relationships, when things have 'run their course,' when things have become untenable. The relationship between my mother and I as blood. The fact that she chewed my food for me as a child. Premastication. That people see premastication as a form of kissing. The bond between mother and child.

She said: *I feel like I could've done more. I felt I was going to lose you. I thought about hospital, but I think it would've broken you. I don't think you could've been away from your family.*

Isn't this just a mother's wishful thinking? Was it really a benefit to me to stay at home? Or, perhaps, was it my mother who could not bear to be away from her son? Perhaps I would have 'got better' quicker, more efficiently had I gone to hospital. Perhaps not.

There are no words. It is difficult to glean answers through the fog and fever of memory.

My mother revealed that she would put things in my food when I wasn't looking. She called this sugar bombing. It was, in many ways, for her, an act of warfare: my mother versus this other version of me, or, what she termed, unconfidently, the 'chemical imbalance.' Every evening she would make me hot chocolates – *the most calorific there was* – and would put so much sugar in it that you *could stand a spoon in it*. I don't remember this because I didn't see it. I wonder what else there was that I didn't see.

She mentioned how every evening she would be throwing food away, throwing it all in the bin and that she panicked. She mentioned that there was, on top of this ordeal, the problem with my grandmother.

*

It is worth noting here that there are some facts and figures that my grandmother and I share, things that I believe are not merely coincidence.

My grandmother, Anne, was born on 19th February, 1921. I share the same birthday as her. When I was born, her husband, Walter – my grandfather, my mother's father – died of a heart attack. I never knew him. I have heard countless stories about him, especially from my Uncle Mike, an uncle I am fond of, a man who has the ability to weave amazing stories from our family's history.

*

The fact that I shared the same birthday as my grandmother is something I remember from an early age. 'Birthday boy,' she would call me in her house in Wolverhampton. She died in a care home not far from that house on 14th February, 2003, five days shy of her 84th birthday. I didn't visit her in the last few months of her life because I was too scared to see her. I was young and immature. I remember going to visit her in the care home and not being able to talk to her. She didn't know who I was. Other times her face would light up as if in acknowledgement, but even this was in doubt.

My grandmother had, according to my mother, vascular dementia. *It was her trip to America*, my mother said. I asked when this was because I couldn't remember. *The early nineties*, my mother said. She went to visit my Aunt in North Carolina and, on the way there, she got deep vein thrombosis. And then, when she returned, my mother said: *She was a completely different person. She never smiled again.*

*

I found this disturbing: that somebody can leave a place as one person and return as another. Sickness as an act of bodies replacing bodies, or like a magic show – somebody entering a box as one thing and leaving as another. I feel this way with my grandmother and myself: we were one self, then we were another self. We changed overnight. My parents lost a son. My mother lost the mother she knew and gained a new mother, a mother she had to reeducate herself in.

I was new to myself too.

The things I thought I knew about myself had changed instantly. Being inside your body is not an unconscious act but, to me, an act of constant reeducation. You learn to adapt. I couldn't eat solid food, so I had to find something. Soups, yoghurts, mousses. I couldn't sit still because of my bodily convulsions so I found secluded areas. I hung out in empty classrooms. Towards the end of my illness, I actually locked myself inside my form room at lunchtimes and ordered as much food as I could from the tuck shop. Beans, toast, hash browns, sausages. Each food required a unique understanding between tongue, throat and texture. The sausage was different because of the skin casing, something I still discard to this day. Beans were difficult at first, but proved to be the easiest to swallow. Carrots were difficult because I seemed to just chew and chew and chew and it never ended.

It was the texture of the food. Some textures work, some don't. This is still true now. Some foods are easier swallowed in seclusion, some better in groups. For example, I can't eat a rump steak at a restaurant because it will just be chewed into a grey ball, which I, more often than not, put into a napkin. Crisps are a great food to eat in groups because although they are sharp and potentially dangerous – a shard, I think, could tear my throat, maybe go down the wrong way – they actually make their presence known in my mouth. I like the confidence of the crisp. You know it is there, in your mouth and you feel it go down your throat. Some foods feel weak, almost as if they are not there at all and this is when things become dangerous. This is when I need liquids to help ease it down my throat. In Louis Elsberg's book on the throat, he mentions that the throat does so much work for the human body, almost a thankless task; but I do not see it this way. I feel my throat needs an intern and that intern is water.

*

There were moments in our life – my mother, my two sisters – that were punctuated by my grandmother's increasingly erratic behaviour. I remember that we would visit my grandmother every evening with a plate of hot food that my mother cooked. My mother cooked for her every night without fail. We would drive the car to her house and knock on the door. I remember the colour of the door and what kind of doorknob it had. I remember the fireplace in the living room, which wasn't really a fireplace but one of those old-fashioned electric heaters, embedded in the hearth, surrounded by mustard-coloured tiles. On the mantelpiece there were family photographs. There was one of my grandmother's sister Kathleen. She was said to have died of a brain haemorrhage. Even then, at a young age, there was talk of bodies and death, of haemorrhages and heart attacks. There was my grandmother's other little sister, her name I forget, who, when she was around nine years old, cut her leg open from a fall. She died. These were the days when people died from cuts and colds and flus.

I remember the television, too. Like the fireplace it was old fashioned and made from wood. You had to turn a dial to change the channel.

Enter the living room and the fireplace was directly in front of you. To the left of the door was a large table and just to the left of that on the left-hand wall was a cabinet where records were kept. There was a record player just underneath and I remember listening to Dinah Washington and Glenn Miller and Buddy Holly. I also think of those three musicians in terms of their deaths, too: Dinah Washington died of a drug overdose at 39; Glenn Miller went missing over the English Channel at 40; Buddy Holly died in a plane crash at 22.

I think back to the photographs on the mantelpiece. These photographs were always a point of reference for us as a family. We would pick one up and talk about it, maybe hear a story about them from the past. *During the Blitz when me and Nelly went out during an air raid. We went to the Civic. We could hear airplanes.* These photographs were windows into a family history, a collective memory. These photographs – taken on a film camera – are carefully chosen moments. These are memories we have chosen to remember.

Only the other day at a birthday party in Clapton, I sat for at least five minutes as a friend of mine captured the 'moment' and then deemed it not good enough: we captured several moments, but I don't believe we captured 'the moment'. I was tagged in the photograph, my name close to her name, but there was no connection here: it was, in fact, just a forced souvenir of an evening. This is the way most nights out, these days: waiting for the moment where we can take the photograph and be done with it all, capture the moment in all its perfection and then breathe a sigh of relief.

*

There was something about these photographs on the mantelpiece that were rich, like food. There were levels to the photograph, levels of life. As a teenager, I often wanted to eat these photographs and digest the history that way. Even upon reading Susan Sontag's essay on photography, I see the phrase 'image-choked world' and think not of too many images, but images literally forcing their way down my oesophagus, the photograph as a piece of food, a desperate way to internalise the photograph, a way of absorbing it in a kind of cannibalistic way, of owning it and all the knowledge that exists in its layers.[2]

*

It is with these photographs that I saw the first signs of my grandmother's illness. She began to turn the photographs around: she thought they were looking at her. She became dismissive of the people in the photographs. These two-dimensional images were, to her, three dimensional. They had eyes. They were watching her and watching us.

Magazines, too, were turned over: images on the front of *Hello* magazine were watching. The gaze of the photograph was real.

*

As my grandmother's illness became more and more pronounced, she was moved to a care home. This was,

[2] Two Kingston University students, Joshua Lake and Luke Evans, swallowed two capsules containing 35mm film so they could take pictures of their insides. Acids and enzymes seeped onto the film and created photographs that looked more like apocalyptic landscapes than something medical.

and I believe still is, a point of contention between my mother's side of the family. But what we all agreed on is the savagery of vascular dementia as a disease. It takes away memories, one by one. I think back to the photographs and the way they, too, went through a form of degeneration. They were, once, a point of reference and a jumping-off point for stories; then they became real human beings, agents of paranoia for my grandmother. And, finally, they lost both their history and their ability to spy on her: they became pieces of paper. The memory of my grandmother seemed like a Polaroid in reverse, the image once existed in all its clarity and, then – in what seemed like minutes – turned milky white, and then disappeared altogether.

*

I find that my memories of the eating disorder are like Polaroids too.

*

Some things I remember about my grandmother: the smell of her urine. Her wrists getting smaller the closer she got to death. The care home.

I do not remember much about the care home except for the hand rails. I remember thinking that hand rails to assist the elderly down hallways were a depressing sight. This is what I think every time I see a handrail now.

*

I remember the house, too. We returned to the house a lot, even when she wasn't in it. The dog still lived in the house. My mother wandered around the house, tidying, hoovering. My mother constantly cleaned that house and she constantly cleans the house she lives in now.

*

The conversation between my mother and I ended at 21:38. That was the first time we had spoken about what happened, at length, for 16 years. We had both been guilty of trying to forget what happened. For me, the act of forgetting was a necessary tool to 'get over' the eating disorder and my fear of choking on food. It is only recently, now that I have started to find it difficult to swallow again, that I realised nothing was overcome. I didn't 'get over' anything.

To add to the idea of a Polaroid, let's think of a metronome ticking back and forth, or me as a teenager rewinding, playing and rewinding the same scene over and over again. This is what happens to the memories: they drift away and then they return. The Polaroid turns to nothing and then, going forward again, the image returns.

Postscript

Around three years have passed since I wrote this essay. I haven't read it since. I'm sitting on my couch now and next to me is a black hat and a book and a wallet. I went back to the warehouse where I used to live on Rendlesham Road and, unfortunately, the garage and the car parts and the condoms have all gone now and have been replaced by a scrap metal yard.

I haven't spoken to anybody in my family about these events since either. I still find it strange that I wrote a series of essays on my eating disorder during this year, 2016, and then never really returned to it. I liked to think that I had got it all out of me, that my body was a toothpaste tube that had been rolled up and every dreg was eked out of me.

This isn't true.

My relationship with food is still a difficult one. I do not eat in front of other people still. The act of eating is still one of solitude, as if I sit at the dinner table with the food itself and that swallowing is a form of dialogue with it.

I lived in Las Vegas for a short period last year and things got considerably worse out there. I couldn't eat properly and then I travelled to Los Angeles and San Francisco. I drank liquids. Blended vegetables and soups. Smoothies. And then upon returning to Vegas again, I couldn't have a dialogue with food. I was stuck.

It took me a while to get over this and now I try not to think about it. My housemate, Alex Widdowson, has been kind enough to listen to my thoughts about eating. It has helped.

I feel it's never over, but now, at 31 years old, I feel more in control than I did when I was young. I was growing up and I found it difficult. I remember waking up most nights and my stomach was screaming. I remember feeling faint every day and angry every day. I rememeber in 2015 a teacher I worked with laughed at the essay and said how trivial it was. Perhaps to her it was. But it wasn't trivial to me. I often wanted to die when I was a young boy and would cry to the point where there was no sound left in me.

One thing that I'd say sticks out from looking back over the essay and seeing myself now is that I still have an uneasy relationship with my body. This is clear in the essay and it is clear, now, to me.